THE CATON OF A CAPTAIN

BEYOND THE ARISTOCRACY

LINDA RAE SANDE

Twisted Teacup
PUBLISHING

The Caton of a Captain

Cover photograph © Period Images.com

Background cover image © DepositPhotos.com

Cover art by Twisted Teacup Publishing

Edited by Katrina Teele-Fair

http://www.lindaraesande.com

ISBN: 978-1-946271-67-9

Twisted Teacup Publishing, Cody, Wyoming

ALSO BY LINDA RAE SANDE

The Daughters of the Aristocracy

The Kiss of a Viscount

The Grace of a Duke

The Seduction of an Earl

The Sons of the Aristocracy

Tuesday Nights

The Widowed Countess

My Fair Groom

The Sisters of the Aristocracy

The Story of a Baron

The Passion of a Marquess

The Desire of a Lady

The Brothers of the Aristocracy

The Love of a Rake

The Caress of a Commander

The Epiphany of an Explorer

The Widows of the Aristocracy

The Gossip of an Earl

The Enigma of a Widow

The Secrets of a Viscount

The Widowers of the Aristocracy

The Dream of a Duchess

The Vision of a Viscountess

The Conundrum of a Clerk

The Charity of a Viscount

The Cousins of the Aristocracy

The Promise of a Gentleman

The Pride of a Gentleman

The Holidays of the Aristocracy

The Christmas of a Countess

The Knot of a Knight

The Heirs of the Aristocracy

The Angel of an Astronomer

The Puzzle of a Bastard

The Choice of a Cavalier

The Bargain of a Baroness

The Jewel of an Earl's Heir

The Vixen of a Viscount

The Honor of an Heir

The Rose of a Sultan's Son

The Ladies of the Aristocracy

The Lady of a Grump

The Lady of a Sultan

The Tulip of a Sultan's Son

The Wager of a Wallflower

Beyond the Aristocracy

The Pleasure of a Pirate

The Making of a Mistress

The Bride of a Baronet

The Caton of a Captain

CHAPTER 1
AN AUCTION

July 1815, Naval auction, Portsmouth, Sussex, England

A cacophony of voices sounded around Captain Edward Poulsen, some speaking English, two speaking German, another arguing in Spanish, and a myriad of other foreign languages adding to the mix inside the makeshift naval auction hall. Outside, a drizzle continued to soak the wooden docks of Portsmouth.

"Our next ship is the 64-gun, two-decker warship, *Caton*. She was built in 1777 and captured from the French," the auctioneer called out. "Owned by the British Navy, this fine specimen saw action and is admittedly in need of some repairs to make her seaworthy."

"She's got a hole in her hull!" someone in the crowd called out. A wave of chuckles swept through those assembled, although Edward wasn't one of those who was amused. He'd been on deck when a French cannonball had breached the hull. At least the comment might dissuade others from bidding on the ship he had commanded for over four years. He'd been its first mate for many years before taking the wheel when the captain had been promoted.

The noise in the hall lessened, and an older gentleman called out, "One-hundred pounds."

Annoyed he hadn't been able to attempt a higher starting bid, the auctioneer sighed. "One-hundred pounds has been bid for a ship that cost over thirty-eight-thousand pounds to build," he called out in a voice tinged with annoyance.

Edward knew if he bid two-hundred pounds, the older gentleman would simply counter the bid. They would shout out numbers back and forth until one of them finally gave up and waited for the next ship to come up for bid.

"One-thousand," Edward called out, which had the small crowd reacting with surprise.

Caught off-guard, the auctioneer stared at Edward. "Sold!" he yelled, not giving anyone else an opportunity to counter the captain's bid.

The noise once again increased as Edward made his way toward the front of the hall. "Did I hear right? You just bought your own ship?"

Edward turned to see his old friend and fellow naval commander, Paul Jacobs, regarding him with a smirk. "It is, but now it's mine," he said with a huge grin. "Why are you here?"

"Thought I'd see what's being sold off," Paul replied as he joined him on the way to the auctioneer's table. "You never know. There might be one I like better than my own *Fate's Destiny*," he went on.

"So privateering is paying off for you?" Edward asked, curious to hear what his friend had to say on the matter. He had struggled with the matter of what he was going to do with his life now that the Napoleonic wars were over. His services to the British Navy were no longer required.

"Pay's far better than being a British naval officer," Paul replied.

"Well, that's good to hear, because privateering is what I'm about to do."

Paul scoffed. "There's plenty of work to go 'round, now that the war is over. I've had to turn down three jobs in just the past month."

Edward's eyes rounded. "Very good to know. Where are you off to next?" he asked.

"Havre. I have some cargo to fetch for a client in Cornwall." He pulled a chronometer from his waistcoat pocket. "I'd best get going. I told my crew we would push off at three of the clock."

Pulling his chronometer from his waistcoat pocket, Edward winced when he saw the time. He had a thought the two might head to a nearby pub for a pint. Learning who might be in need of a privateer would give him an advantage when repairs on the *Caton* were complete. "Well, may the wind be with you," he said as he shook hands with the other captain.

"And with you." Jacobs disappeared in the crowd as Edward faced the auctioneer's staff.

"Only buying the one ship today?" a middle-aged man asked from behind the cluttered table, his manner suggesting his purchase was more bother than it was worth his time.

"Aye," Edward replied, pulling his purse from inside his topcoat pocket. At first, he thought the man was joking, but he remembered the number of bidders who had been calling out bids on more than one ship. Agents from shipping companies, no doubt, charged with acquiring multiple ships to expand their fleets.

"That will be one-thousand pounds plus forty for the papers."

Edward bristled at having to pay extra for the documentation to prove he owned the ship. "Where can I find her?" has asked as he signed a series of papers. When he'd last limped into port two months prior—the damage from the cannonball was high enough up that the *Caton* hadn't sunk into the Channel—he had left it in a berth near the repair yards. When he'd walked past that area earlier that morning, the ship wasn't there.

The auctioneer's assistant pulled a paper from a stack in front of him and frowned. "She should be in dry dock," he murmured. "Hull's got a hole, and she'll need a scraping," he added, referring to the barnacles that probably covered the entire bottom of the ship. "But according to this, she's in berth seven," he said as he handed the final paper to Edward. "Sign at the bottom."

Edward signed the paper and handed it back along with a wad of bank notes. "I'll need proof of ownership," he said.

"Right here," the clerk said as he gave him a sheaf of papers. "If you're boarded, show this," he said as he pointed to the paper on top.

"How long can she stay where she is?" Edward asked, his attention on the papers.

"Naval operations is requesting ships be claimed within the week," the clerk replied. "Unless you're employing them for repairs, then you'll want to see the crew chief."

"Seems fair," Edward replied. Although he knew several shipbuilders who worked in the naval yard at Portsmouth, he wasn't certain he would use their services. Enough former naval men had banded together and gone into business for themselves doing repairs that he thought to employ one of the new companies to do the work on the hull. He also wanted the *Caton* painted and its new moniker added—*Black Cat.*

"Navy wants to know what you intend to do with the

ship, Captain," the clerk said as he consulted a checklist. "With a reminder that you cannot use it for smuggling."

Edward bristled at the implication that he would be using the warship he had commanded for over four years to smuggle contraband. "I'm a privateer now," he stated. "My ship will be available for hire unless I'm already transporting legitimate cargo."

The clerk nodded. "Very good, Captain."

Edward turned to take his leave, nearly colliding with the gentleman who had opened the bidding on the *Caton*.

CHAPTER 2
AN OFFER

*D*ressed in a topcoat made of navy superfine and wearing Nankeen breeches and a red waistcoat, the middle-aged man smelled of fine cologne. He held a silver-topped cane in one gloved hand, but obviously didn't need it to walk. A beaver top hat was tucked under the same arm that held the cane.

"Pardon, sir," Edward said, attempting to move around the man.

"Arthur Pendragon," the man said, holding out his right hand. "Pendragon Imports."

Edward blinked and belatedly shook the man's hand, about to make a joke of the man's name. Did his parents really name him after the fabled king of the round table? "Captain Poulsen," he countered.

"I take it you have a history with the *Caton*?"

Realizing he wasn't going to be able to leave without answering the gentleman, Edward said, "I was her captain, yes," he replied. "Four years, and her first mate before that."

"We'd like to hire you," Pendragon stated.

Edward furrowed a brow. "My ship isn't even seaworthy," he said. "I expect it will be a fortnight or more before she is."

"That's fine," Pendragon replied. "The timeline works perfectly for our needs."

Curious as to what the importer's needs might be, Edward's gaze darted about to ensure no one was eavesdropping on their conversation. "And what might those needs be?" he countered, indicating they should move to quieter environs. The auction hall was once again noisy with the excitement around the current offering, a three-decker gunship, bids and counter bids shouted out faster than the auctioneer could acknowledge.

Once outside the auction hall, a young man ran up to stand next to Pendragon, an umbrella opened and held up to shield the man from the continuing drizzle.

"Although we're involved in transporting a number of goods from half a dozen countries, we are in need of a ship to import brandy from France," Pendragon explained.

"Brandy?" Edward repeated. "Isn't that illegal?"

"It was," Pendragon replied. "Now... perfectly legal, as long as it goes through the proper channels."

Even as the gentleman said the words, Edward stiffened. For some reason, he didn't believe Pendragon Imports would be using 'proper channels' to bring the stuff into England. "And where might those channels be?"

"Have you ever heard of Swain Cove?" Pendragon asked as they entered the public house that was closest to the docks. The odor of unwashed bodies, stale ale, and fresh baked bread assaulted their nostrils.

"Cornwall?" Edward guessed, not surprised when the young man with the umbrella moved to the tap and saw to placing an order.

"Indeed. We've just hired a company there to see to properly preparing the brandy for transport to London."

They took seats at a table for two. "Properly preparing?" Edward repeated. He scoffed and rolled his eyes.

"Well it doesn't come out of France ready to drink," Pendragon stated. "Unless you have a want to die of alcohol poisoning." He shed his top hat and leather gloves onto the table.

Edward winced. "I'm sure I wouldn't know. I am not a connoisseur of liquors. I tend to drink ale." At one time, he had enjoyed a brandy or two with his older brother on rainy days in London, the liquor providing as much warmth as the fire they were sitting next to in the study. He had a brief thought he should pay a call on his brother before beginning his next career, but he shook off the thought in favor of concentrating on the importer's words.

Pendragon nodded. "Well, first, it must be let down. It must be colored with caramel syrup. And then it must be put into oak barrels for transport," he explained.

"Let down?" Edward repeated, not surprised when a tavern wench set down two tankards of ale and a huge platter of sliced meats and cheeses. A loaf of bread followed, delivered by a much younger woman who dipped a curtsy as she placed linen napkins on their laps and batted her lashes.

"Hungry?" Pendragon asked, indicating the food. "Help yourself." He handed the server a coin, and she grinned.

"If you need more, guv'nor, just wave," she said, arching a blonde brow.

Pendragon cleared his throat and ignored her implication. "Could you bring us two glasses of brandy?" he asked her. "And warm the glasses first?"

She blinked. "Right away, guv'nor," she said as she dipped a curtsy and hurried off to the tap.

"As for the letting down," Pendragon continued as he leaned forward. "Brandy comes in tubs—"

"Half ankers, are they not?" Edward asked, remembering having seen hundreds of them when he was last on a dock in France.

"Yes. And about seventy points over proof."

Edward's eyes widened. "That's one way to get drunk quick," he murmured, now understanding Pendragon's reference to alcohol poisoning.

"Which is why it has to have distilled water added," Pendragon said at the same moment the wench returned with the glasses of brandy.

He gave her another coin and then held up one of the glasses. "Brandy is not this color naturally."

Edward watched the server move off to another table before his attention settled on the glass. "What color is it?"

"Sort of the color of straw when it comes out of the still pot," Pendragon replied as he swirled the brandy in the glass.

"Straw?" Edward repeated, his brows furrowing in a grimace.

"Your reaction explains why caramel syrup must be added. To make it dark. To make it appear expensive."

"Changes the flavor, I suppose?" Edward guessed. He had seen liquors with so much alcohol, they appeared to have fumes rising above the surface, and they had tasted almost as bad as he imagined kerosene would.

"No. Never," Pendragon countered. "The caramel must never change the brandy other than in color, which means it cannot be burnt, and it cannot be too overcooked."

Intrigued, Edward held up his own glass of brandy and took an experimental sniff. "And this company you have in Cornwall...?"

"They are masters at preparing liquors," Pendragon stated. "Once you deliver the tubs, they take over, and then my transport company sees to delivering the final barrels to London."

"Legitimately?" Edward asked, still not convinced the operation would be overseen by excisemen or revenue agents.

"Legitimately," Pendragon affirmed. "A thousand tubs imported. One-thousand tubs sent off to London. Are you interested?"

Inhaling softly, Edward realized he had the opportunity to be involved with a business that would no doubt be successful. Pendragon's manner of speech and dress and the coin he had already dropped during the past hour were proof that he was wealthy.

"When and where would I make the pick up? I doubt I can take a thousand tubs at one time, though." He attempted a quick calculation in his head as to how many tubs might fit in the cargo hold of the *Caton*.

"Cherbourg-en-Cotentin," Pendragon replied, referring to a French port that was the closest to Cornwall. "Four weeks from now. Say we start with two-hundred tubs? I'll pay you half when it's loaded and the rest when you deliver it to Swain Cove."

Two-hundred tubs would fit in the cargo hold with room to spare. Pendragon obviously knew that when he bid on the *Caton*. "How often?"

Pendragon shrugged. "Every fortnight?"

"That's a lot of brandy," Edward said as he examined the glass of the liquor that had been set before him. Holding it in front of the candle lamp in the middle of their table, he could see through the dark amber liquid. He sniffed it again, detecting a hint of oak. When he took a sip, he felt it burn as it slid down his throat.

"This one is not very good," Pendragon remarked

dryly. "Probably above proof, which means whoever made it didn't use the proper instrument to gauge its strength."

Edward took another sip, deciding there was a hint of smoke he hadn't detected before. His belly felt especially warm, though, as if the brandy was burning a hole in it. "What instrument might that be?"

"A hydrometer," Pendragon replied, grimacing upon trying another sip of his brandy. "Parliament requires brandy be no more than forty-nine pounds of alcohol to fifty-one pounds of water. I would say this one is the other way around or worse."

"Doesn't the stuff have to age?" Edward asked as he helped himself to some of the food. Although he hadn't intended to eat with the gentleman, he would feel the effects of the above proof brandy if he didn't put something in his stomach.

"At least two years," Pendragon acknowledged. "Most of what you'll be transporting will have aged in oak casks for between four and six years. Hopefully longer. I'm still working with my supplier there. Now that Napoleon has been defeated, restrictions should ease up a bit."

When the importer mentioned how much he would pay for the *Caton's* services, Edward realized he could cover the cost of his ship, the repairs to the hull, and pay a full crew after only two trips across the Channel. "How do I contact you when my ship is ready?"

Pendragon pulled a card from his waistcoat pocket. "Here's the address to send a missive. Let me know when you can be in Cherbourg-en-Cotentin, and I will meet you there. If it's all right with you, I'll come aboard and direct the off-loading once you're anchored in Swain Cover."

Edward studied the bright white pasteboard, noting the engraved words. The two spoke for a few more minutes, discussing further terms and the manner of payment. "Very well. I thank you for the meal," Edward said as he gathered his tricorn hat and greatcoat. "I'm off to find my ship. See you in a couple of weeks." He shook hands with Pendragon and then took his leave of the public house.

CHAPTER 3
A CREW

The drizzle had ceased by the time Edward made his way back to the docks of Portsmouth. Despite nearly every berth taken up with a British naval ship, only a few workers were on the docks.

Berth seven was where he had left the *Caton* the month before, heartened the damaged ship had managed to survive long enough to bring her captain and crew back to British shores. Napoleon's navy might have made the hole in the hull with a well-aimed cannonball, but the *Caton* hadn't sunk.

Having delivered its cargo of artillery to a naval outpost in the Kingdom of the Netherlands and dispatched most of its own cannon shot in the battle against a French frigate, the *Caton* was running light when it docked. The damage remained well above the water line, and Edward hoped it had stayed that way.

"Can I help you, sir?" an ensign asked from behind him.

Edward turned at hearing the familiar voice. "Ensign Streater?" he replied, a grin replacing his dour expression.

"Captain Poulsen. Never thought to see you back

here," Ensign Streater said as he shook hands with his former commander.

"Came to claim my ship and arrange for repairs," Edward explained. "I just bought her at auction."

George Streater's eyes rounded. "Well, congratulations, Captain. What are you going to use her for, if you don't mind me asking?"

Remembering he would have had to be vague had the ensign asked earlier that day, Edward now realized he could announce his new position. "Transporting brandy from France to start," he replied. "I'm going into business as a privateer."

A huge grin revealed the ensign's complete set of teeth as well a dimple that youthened him even more than his blond hair, freckles, and sixteen years. He had spent eight of those aboard navy ships. "Can I join you, Captain? Be part of your crew?"

Edward gave a start. "What about the British Navy?" he countered. "You're on track for a ship of your own in ten years or so."

George shook his head. "Navy doesn't need me any more," he replied as one shoulder lifted in a shrug. "War's over—"

"For now," Edward countered. With Britain having been at war with some other country almost continuously since the time of his birth, he knew it wouldn't be long before the British Navy would be dispatched again.

The ensign shrugged. "My last day is the end of the month."

"Well, then I suppose you'll be the first crewman I hire for the *Black Cat*," Edward stated.

"The *Black Cat*?" The ensign's eyes rounded.

"New name of the *Caton*," Edward said. "But first, I have to get her repaired. Who's the best and where can I find 'em?"

Waving to a building at the edge of the dock, George said, "There's a repair crew in there that won't cheat you, Captain. All former navy men. Got let go like me, so they started up their own concern and are looking for clients."

Edward followed the ensign's line of sight and nodded once he found the shingle on the front of the building that looked like a wharfside warehouse. "Thanks for the tip. When you're done with your current assignment, find a cabin onboard—not mine—and make yourself at home," he ordered.

"Aye, Captain. Thank you."

With that, Edward headed off to arrange repairs. Having acquired a ship, a job, and the start of a crew, he felt as if he was ready to take on the world. Or at least a small part of it.

CHAPTER 4
CARAMEL SYRUP

A few days later, in Swain Cove, Cornwall

Glancing around the market square of Swain Cove, Catherine Bristow decided her weekly shopping was complete. She had managed to visit each and every stall, buying a little here, a little there, and a lot from the one man who offered sugar for sale.

If only Felix Odenkirk wasn't such an odious brute.

"You know, if you married me, I wouldn't charge ye so much for the sugar," he said as he placed the ten-pound sack of sugar in her basket. She was fairly sure it was less than ten pounds. Closer to nine if she could trust her measuring bowls.

Pretending innocence, she batted her lashes and claimed she was much too young to marry. "Besides, me father won't let me," she said with a shrug. "Needs me, he does."

This last was true. Her father needed her to help with his confectionery business, and if she had to choose between the marriage and her father, she would choose Franklin Bristow every time.

That didn't mean she had given up on marriage. Her

expectations were high, though. She wanted a handsome man. Employed and respected. One who valued her for what she could provide in a marriage, and not just children or delicious dinners.

She could create candies. Sweets and caramels. A dozen different kinds of comfits, if she had the right ingredients. Delectable delights that would have her husband hurrying home to her every night.

The odor of burnt sugar had Catherine's nose wrinkling as she entered her family's business, *Caramel and Sons.* There might not be any sons about—she had been the only offspring of Katrina and Franklin Bristow—but appearances were paramount.

"The temperature is too high!" she called out, not sure who would be cooking the water and sugar mixture to make caramel syrup at that time of the morning.

"Damn stove. Can't control this heat," she heard her father curse from the kitchen.

Sighing, she removed her redingote and hurried to join him, hoping the batch wasn't completely ruined. Sugar was expensive. She had paid more for sugar that morning than she had ever paid before.

"Inflation," the brute had said when he practically tossed the ten-pound sack of sugar into her worn basket.

Bastard.

"Here, let me," Catherine said as she took the giant wooden paddle from her father and began stirring in earnest.

"Where have you been?" Franklin asked as he stepped back from the Castrol stove, annoyance evident in his voice.

"It's market day, Father. Someone has to do the shopping," Catherine replied as she moved the pan off the iron plate. From the heat that radiated from the brick-and-mortar stove, she knew her father had put far too much wood in the chamber. "I brought more sugar."

"Sorry. I forgot," her father replied as he blew his nose into a linen handkerchief. "I panicked. Heard from that bloke again. About the brandy."

Catherine stilled her movements. That bloke her father seemed so upset about might be their way of making a go of their burgeoning candy business. No one in this part of Cornwall seemed particularly interested in hard candies and caramels, but their ability to make caramel syrup had attracted the attentions of those who wanted to import distilled spirits. Although they had been successful in adding it to a batch of experimental scotch from up north—the natural color was apparently too light to suit those who were trying the liquor for the first time —the distillers had elected to use a different company closer to their operation for future batches.

The experience had been invaluable, though. Catherine had learned how to not only make caramel syrup that didn't change the flavor of the scotch, she had sorted how to make it possible to thin the syrup with scotch first to make it easier to mix it in as a coloring. A little more work on the front end made it much easier to do the coloring on the back end.

"You could have distilled some more water," she suggested. "We'll need much more of it than we will syrup when it comes to brandy." She used a lever to raise the kettle higher above the flame. "Did he give you a date when the tubs will be delivered?" she added, sighing with relief when she saw no evidence of burned sugar at the bottom of the kettle. She scraped the bottom with the paddle again, just to be sure.

"End of the month. His missive says he found a sea captain with a ship that can bring two-hundred tubs to start."

Catherine blinked. "To *start*?" she repeated. She mentally calculated how much liquor that would be. "Father, that could be as much as eight-hundred gallons of brandy," she said in awe. She glanced around the kitchen. "It's going to have to be let down before we add the syrup. We're going to need more pots. Lots more pots, with spouts, and casks, too."

"I know, I know," Franklin replied. "I sent an order to Acme in Stoke-on-Trent last week. Think I might have to double it, though. "

Catherine winced. Why couldn't the pottery capital of England be closer to Cornwall? "Is he going to supply the casks for shipping?" Catherine asked, her efforts at stirring becoming more labored. The caramel was thickening nicely, the surface bubbles lazily breaking in loud plops. She eyed the tub of brandy Arthur Pendragon had left in their care the week before. She had already added the required amount of distilled water to bring it to proper proof.

"He assured me he would see to that part of it," her father replied.

"Good. I need some of that brandy. To thin this down," she said.

"But... but that just needs coloring," her father argued.

"Please, Father. I know what I'm doing," she countered, continuing to stir despite having extinguished the flame beneath the pot.

"How much?"

"Start pouring. Slowly. I'll tell you when to stop," she instructed. "But we do need to measure how much we've used so we can do it again."

She winced when the first of the stream of pale gold brandy hit the hot caramel syrup, the liquid bubbling and hissing. She could practically smell the alcohol burning off the brandy. After a few seconds, though, the brandy began to incorporate as she stirred the syrup.

"Surely that's enough," her father murmured, worry in his voice.

"Not yet," she replied, continuing to stir. "We want it easily stirrable once it goes into the let down brandy." In fact, if the brandy had to be transported over land for any distance, the movement alone would do the stirring for them. They would only have to add the syrup to the casks before they were sealed for transport. They still had to determine exactly how much to add, though.

"Now?" he asked again, his brows furrowing in worry as he watched the thin stream of brandy disappear into the syrup.

"Keep going," she replied. "We're close."

"It's half gone," he complained, pulling the cask of brandy from the edge of the kettle.

"Father," she scolded. "It's not as if you were going to drink the entire tub."

Franklin's expression suggested that he had indeed counted on imbibing most, if not all, of the experimental batch of brandy. "Thought I could sell some to the *Cock and Bull*," he countered, referring to the local tavern. "Maybe some to the *Mermaid's Rest*."

Catherine scoffed. "As if there is anyone in this town who would appreciate a fine glass of brandy," she murmured.

"I would," he replied as he straightened.

"All right, you can stop now, but don't go far," she said as she stirred the thinned concoction. "This is as thick as this is going to get," she said as she pulled the paddle from the syrup and allowed it to drip from the spoon.

"Liquid gold," her father murmured happily.

"A bit more brandy," she ordered.

Her father rolled his eyes and added a splash more to the kettle. "Should I taste it?" he asked.

"Maybe," she hedged. "But remember, it's not supposed to change the flavor of the brandy. Mr. Pendragon was very insistent that it not taste of caramel or of burnt sugar."

He dipped a tasting spoon into the syrup and waited a moment for it to cool before he stuck it in his mouth.

"Well?"

"Like you said, it doesn't have much in the way of flavor," he said with some disappointment.

Catherine had already started her own tasting, frowning at first and then visibly relaxing on her second try. "How much brandy did you add?"

Gauging the amount based on what was left in the cask, Franklin cursed softly. "Three gallons."

"And how much sugar and how much water did you use?" she asked, ready to record the recipe for future batches.

Franklin's mouth opened and then closed.

"You did take note of the amounts?" she pressed.

Instead of answering, her father sighed and moved to a shelf. He pulled out a measuring bowl. "I filled this first with the sugar to here, and then to the same line with the water."

Her brows rising appreciatively, Caroline grinned. "Very good, Father. I'll make a note of it for when we have to make more."

"More?" he repeated. "Don't you think there's enough there for two-hundred tubs?"

"Probably enough for twice that," she agreed, "but if Mr. Pendragon has us do one-thousand tubs, we'll need more."

"That's a lot of sugar," he countered.

"And a lot of distilled water," she said with an arched brow.

"I'll get on it right away," he replied, moving off to the area where a series of glass tubes, flasks and a huge tank of water were located.

Catherine watched him go, wincing at seeing how stooped he had become in the past few years, the years since her mother's death from a fever. Franklin Bristow had teased several times that he would acquire another wife as good or better than Katrina Laurent Bristow, but in truth, he wasn't even looking, let alone courting anyone.

Catherine's thoughts once again conjured her handsome man. There wasn't another like him in Swain Cove, for none of the men she knew in the small community were as tall or had shoulders as broad as his. None had his dark hair or easy smile, nor teeth that had been bestowed by the dental gods. None but him would be allowed to remove her slippers and stockings, let alone her gown and corset.

After that, she wasn't sure what her handsome man would do to her—her mother hadn't lived long enough to explain what a man did with a naked woman, but she certainly liked the thought of his hands on her bare skin, his warm breath on her shoulder, his lips on hers.

She spent the rest of the afternoon thinking of her handsome man as she cleaned up and prepared pots for distilled water. For a time, she tried to think of a good name for him. Something that sounded strong. Manly. Royal.

She winced.

She didn't want a royal. She didn't even want an aristocrat, although there was one in the area. Viscount Tobias Pencarrow owned Swain Cove and the surrounding environs. He also knew Swain Cove's secrets.

All of them.

His recent inheritance of the title from a father who had ignored the illegal smuggling taking place in the small village might have meant an end to their way of life. An end to the livelihoods of most all who lived in Swain Cove. He could have ordered the smuggling to cease.

But he hadn't.

Although *Caramel and Sons'* business didn't involve anything illegal—at least, not that Catherine was aware—there could come a time when they might have to help someone else by hiding goods in their candy shipments.

Or hiding goods inside of candy.

Catherine nearly giggled at the thought of encasing some small bauble inside of a hard candy or wrapping it with a layer of caramel, its only way out by the mouth of someone who had to suck on the candy until its treasure emerged.

Surely there were easier means to smuggle goods out of Swain Cove. For now, she was happy to simply imagine her handsome man while she distilled gallons of water and boiled sugar into fine candies.

CHAPTER 5
AN AUNT BEARS BAD NEWS

Three days later, Plymouth, Cornwall, England
Before leaving Portsmouth for what he hoped would be a quick trip to Plymouth, Edward appointed Ensign Streater to oversee the repairs and the painting of the *Caton*. He also asked his new first mate to be on the lookout for a few crew members.

Edward had already arranged for new sails to be sewn for the *Caton*.

Black sails.

The sailmaker in Portsmouth had charged him more for them than he charged for white sails, but he also admitted they would last longer. Black sails would also allow the *Black Cat* to travel at night without being easily seen. Although he had no intention of carrying smuggled goods, as a privateer, Edward wanted to ensure he wasn't easily spotted on the water by pirates.

When his arrangements were complete, he caught a mail coach headed west.

Although Swain Cove was two-hundred miles from the naval shipyards at Portsmouth, Edward had a thought to meet those to whom he would be handing off his first delivery of brandy later that month.

According to Arthur Pendragon, the brandy was destined for a candy manufacturer.

Sure *Caramel and Sons* was a front for some sort of illegal operation, Edward had been about to back out of his deal with Pendragon. But once the gentleman explained the need for caramel syrup and distilled water to complete the brandy for shipment, Edward had relaxed.

The very last thing he wanted was to be involved with a smuggling operation.

"Fear not, Captain," Pendragon had said upon their most recent parting. They had nearly run into each other when Pendragon had exited his hotel two days prior, and a quick consult whilst walking to his next destination—a bank—had allowed Edward to ask some pointed questions. "The brandy will be overseen by revenue agents who work in a village near Swain Cove. This is a legitimate concern," Pendragon assured him.

Edward decided he wanted to find out the details for himself. He also needed more men for his crew, and he knew at least three of the former crew of the *Caton* had settled near Plymouth after the war was over.

One of the stops along the mail coach route, Plymouth afforded him a decent place to spend a night while he did what he could to recruit a navigator, a boatswain, and a cook. He wasn't surprised when all three took him up on his offer of employment. None had managed to secure positions worthy of their skills, although the cook was under consideration for a job with a gambling den.

Assured they would all be in Portsmouth prior to the maiden voyage of the *Black Cat*, Edward resumed his trek west on the next day's mail coach.

. . .

The matron who stepped aboard the coach in Exeter brought with her the odor of perfume and the haughty air of entitlement. Her broad hat sported an ostrich feather that bent at an odd angle against the roof of the mail coach.

Pretending to be asleep, Edward heard her scoff of disgust and finally opened one eye to find her staring at him.

"Is there a problem, ma'am?" he asked in a quiet voice, straightening on the bench.

"You might have acknowledged me," she replied in a huff.

Edward opened his other eye, his brow furrowing in confusion. "Ma'am?" he countered in confusion.

"Eddie," she admonished him. "Surely you remember me?"

For a moment, Edward wondered if she might have been one of his brief encounters while he enjoyed shore leave in a seaside port. But she was dressed far too fine to be a prostitute. She was also far older than those he usually engaged for quick tumbles.

Sudden recognition had him straightening even more. "Aunt Theodosia?" he asked in alarm.

"Well, who else would I be?" she replied with a scoff. "It hasn't been *that* long since we saw one another. Has it?"

Edward did a quick mental calculation and arched a dark brow. "Seven years," he claimed. "At the townhouse in London."

Her mouth formed an 'o' before she raised a gloved hand to cover it. "Oh, dear, has it been that long? Wherever have you *been*?"

"At war," he replied with a shrug, wondering how it was his father's sister, a gossip monger, could be so oblivious when it came to world events. "I'm done with the Navy, though. Just bought my own ship. I'm a privateer now," he explained.

"Oh, how exciting," she murmured, even as she seemed confused by his answer.

"I hope not," he countered. "I accepted my first transport job a week ago, and while my ship is being painted, I thought I would meet the people I'm to deliver the goods to," he explained. Edward knew if he didn't give his aunt all the details up front, she would ask a dozen questions in an effort to learn everything she could.

She was a busybody.

"Swain Cove?" she guessed.

Edward's brows arched. "Why, yes. How did you know?"

"Well, where else would a privateer be taking illicit goods?" she asked in a delighted whisper.

"Aunt Theo," he admonished her. "I assure you my business there is entirely legitimate."

She waved a gloved hand. "From the mouths of babes," she teased.

Ignoring her jibe, he asked, "Where are you off to? I didn't know you had settled in Exeter."

Giving him a grin, she leaned over and said, "Who says I settled in Exeter? I actually live not far from Swain Cove."

"Oh?" he asked, alarm once again skittering up his spine. "By yourself?" As far as he knew, Aunt Theodosia had never been married.

"Not exactly," she hedged. "But just you never mind about that little detail."

"Auntie?" he said as both boots landed on the floor of the coach with a *thud*.

"Oh, if you must know, I've been seeing a gentleman in St. Austell. An exciseman," she explained in a quiet voice, her gaze taking in the three other passengers in the coach. Two were apparently sound asleep while an older gentleman had his attention on a week-old copy of *The Times.*

"A revenue agent?" Edward asked, managing to keep his immediate displeasure from sounding in his voice. "For how long?"

Theodosia pretended to think on it for a time before she said, "Five years, I suppose."

Five years? "And he hasn't made you his wife yet?" he asked, not bothering to censure his response. Had his aunt been twenty years younger, she would have been considered a thoroughly ruined woman.

She scoffed. "He's tried. Asked many a time," she replied coyly, stripping a glove off her right hand to display a rather large sapphire gemstone on a gold band. "I finally said I would marry him, but we've not yet set a date."

Edward's eyes widened upon seeing the ring. The gemstone was huge, which had him wondering whether the ring had been purchased in Ludgate Hill or seized during a raid on some smugglers. Then his eyes narrowed. "Are you ever going to set a date?" he asked, suspicious.

"Now that's none of your business, young man," she replied on a huff.

"So... what were you doing in Exeter?" he asked in suspicion.

Theodosia looked as if she might roll her eyes. "My modiste is located there."

"You travel..." Edward took a moment to mentally calculate the distance between St. Austell and Exeter. "*Seventy* miles for a modiste?" he asked in surprise.

Regarding him as if he had lost his mind, Theodosia lifted a shoulder. "Seventy miles is certainly better than going all the way to Oxford Street in London," she reasoned.

Edward blinked, but couldn't argue with her reasoning. "What news do you have from the family?" he asked, deciding it best he change the subject. "I haven't heard from my brother in an age."

Theodosia immediately sobered. "Did the Navy not tell you?" she asked in a quiet voice.

Alarm skittered up Edward's spine. "Tell me what?"

Her eyes rounded before she turned away from him. She blinked her eyes several times and pulled a hanky from a pocket in her redingote.

"Tell me what?" he repeated, struggling to keep his voice down.

"He and your father died... oh, it's been at least a month ago," she whispered. "A terrible fever. Your mother had it, too, but she survived. She's still in London with your sister. At the townhouse in Mayfair. No doubt waiting for your arrival."

Edward swallowed. "Fever," he whispered. "Henry, too?" he asked, referring to his older brother. The heir apparent to a barontage, Henry had been groomed his entire life to take their father's seat in Parliament and to run their modest lands in West Sussex.

"He died first, and I think your father just lost his will to live. He died the following week," she explained. "I'm so sorry you had to learn it from me," Theodosia said on a sigh. "You're the Baron Poulsen now."

The second comment rankled as much as the first comment had Edward struggling with his sorrow. Although he had never been his father's favorite—he was the second son, merely the spare heir—Edward had been good friends with Henry. He never begrudged Henry his eventual title, and truth be told, as the second son, he had always looked forward to a military career.

"I'll have to arrange a man of business," Edward murmured, realizing someone would have to oversee the lands and the tenants who farmed them, see to it bills were paid for the house in Mayfair and the country estate in Sussex.

"The man your father employed has stayed on in the position," Theodosia said. "Your mother insisted until you could return to London and decide what to do."

Relieved to hear it, Edward nodded his understanding. "I wrote to Mother last week when I arrived in Portsmouth," he said. "Surely she'll realize I hadn't yet learned the news. I'll write to her whilst I'm on this trip. Let her know she has done the right thing," he said, still struggling with his sorrow.

"And then you'll go to London?" Theodosia prompted.

He regarded her with a furrowed brow. "I have a contract I must complete," he replied. "I've made a promise I must keep, and I really should see to it before I go to London." Despite his new position, people were already counting on him. He had half of a ship's crew to pay. A contract to fulfill.

About to put voice to a protest, Theodosia sighed and then nodded. "Of course," she finally replied. "No one can ever accuse a Poulsen of breaking a contract," she added, censure evident in her voice.

Although her words suggested he would be forgiven his decision to finish his duty to Pendragon Imports before beginning a new one, Edward couldn't help the feeling that he was no longer held high in her regard.

They traveled in silence the rest of the way to St. Austell.

CHAPTER 6
A BARON ARRIVES

he following afternoon, Swain Cove, Cornwall
Stiff and sore and still smarting from his aunt's news about his father and brother, Edward accepted his valise from the hackney driver and glanced around the main street of Swain Cove.

He had been relieved when the mail coach stopped in St. Austell, allowing him to ensure Aunt Theodosia was met by her betrothed. The gentleman seemed relieved to see her, even when her trunk was dumped at his feet by the coach driver.

"Oh, Timothy. I've an entire new wardrobe for the next six months or so," she had said with a happy grin before the exciseman took her in his arms and kissed her quite thoroughly.

"I'm never letting you out of my sight for that long ever again," Timothy Christianson said when he came up for air.

At seeing Edward's embarrassment—the captain had done his best to ignore the public display of affection—Timothy regarded Edward with a look of contrition before his chest puffed out and his manner turned serious.

"If you're thinking to challenge me over Miss Poulsen, I'll have you know I'm a crack shot, and I can handle a sword."

Edward blinked at the sudden change in the man. One moment, he thought his aunt's paramour a dandy, and the next, he paid witness to a hint of cruelty in the exciseman. "Oh, you misunderstand, sir. Miss Poulsen is my aunt. I merely helped her off the coach." He turned to Theodosia and kissed her on the cheek. "Are you sure you wish me to leave you in his care?" he asked in a hoarse whisper.

"His bark is bigger than his bite. Usually," she replied with a wink and a grin of delight before she sobered. "Do get yourself to London as soon as you can, Lord Poulsen," she added with an exaggerated sigh.

"I will," he promised, wincing at her use of his new title. With a nod to the exciseman—he didn't even wait for an introduction—he returned to the mail coach and took possession of his valise.

"Where can I find transportation to Swain Cove?" he asked the driver.

"There's a hackney that can take you most of the way," the driver replied, pointing to a black carriage that had seen better days. "From there... hire a horse or walk."

The half-hour to Swain Cove seemed to take forever —the hackney driver had accepted a small bribe to take him all the way to the village—and now that he was actually *in* Swain Cove, he almost wished he wasn't. Apparently, the driver noticed his hesitation, for he said, "Ye can arrange a room at the *Cock and Bull*." The driver pointed a pudgy finger toward a Tudor-era tavern in what appeared to be the center of the small village.

"Much obliged," Edward replied. "When does the next mail coach go east?"

"Day after tomorrow, when it heads back from

Penzance. But... you might have an easier time catching a ride on a ship going that way."

"Thanks," Edward replied, his gaze going to the water at the base of Swain Cove. Given the shape of the beach, the cove was hidden from the Channel unless a ship was coming from the west. Only a few fishing vessels were moored at the small docks at the base of the short cliffs. There was a larger vessel tucked into the cove, a two-master that looked as if it might have been left there to rot. There was no sign of life on its decks.

"A hundred pounds, and she's yours," a voice said from behind him.

Edward turned to find a gentleman regarding him with suspicion. Dressed in clothes typical of a member of the gentry—a dark wool topcoat, a hunter green waistcoat, and Nankeen breeches tucked into a pair of what might have been Hoby's—the man wouldn't have looked out of place in Mayfair except his hair looked as if it was in need of a trim. There was something familiar about him, but Edward couldn't place where he might have seen him before. "Oh, I've already got one of my own," he replied.

The man frowned, his gaze sweeping the cove. "Where'd you leave her?"

Giving his head a quick shake, Edward said, "Portsmouth. She's undergoing repairs." He held out his right hand. "Edward Poulsen. Captain of the former British naval ship, *Caton*."

"Tobias Pencarrow," the gentleman replied as his shook his hand. "What's a man without his ship doing all the way down here?"

Edward glanced around, his presence obviously causing some concern with the villagers who passed by. Given the size of it, he supposed any strangers were viewed with suspicion. "I'm doing a bit of reconnoitering," he admitted. He wasn't surprised to see Pencarrow stiffening where he stood. "I'm here to meet the man who runs *Caramel and Sons*. It's about a shipment of brandy I'll be delivering at the end of the month."

Pencarrow seemed to relax some. "Franklin Bristow owns it, but..." His comment trailed off. "Catherine Bristow is who you'll want to speak with," he said in a quieter voice. His brows arched as if to emphasize his recommendation.

"Wife?" Edward guessed, wondering what might be wrong with the owner.

"Daughter, actually, but she's the real reason they're still in business." Pencarrow glanced toward the *Cock and Bull*. "You obviously plan to spend the night."

"I do. I need a room," Edward acknowledged. "I need to wash up a bit, too. Been on a mail coach for a couple of days."

Tobias chuckled. "Well, let's get you a room along with a pint, and then I can take you to meet Miss Bristow."

Edward wondered at the man's willingness to help him. "Much obliged," he said.

The two headed off to the *Cock and Bull* tavern. Given the time of day, only a few villagers were seated at the trestles that filled the public room. A barkeep manned the tap, but Tobias led Edward past him to a small office.

Edward was glad of the escort. Those in the tavern seemed to respect Tobias, and the fact that he was leading a stranger through their midst didn't seem to matter. In fact, many acknowledged Tobias as if they worked for him. "What is it you do here?" Edward asked before they passed the tap.

"I try to keep everyone out of trouble."

It was then Edward realized how he knew Tobias Pencarrow. Not from having the met the man before, but from his name. "You're a viscount," he stated, at the same moment the tavern owner greeted them.

"Cadan Thomas, this is Captain Poulsen. Needs a room for the night and some washing water, if you've got someone who can deliver it."

"Right away, m'lord," Cadan said with a curt nod. He handed Edward a key with a huge leather fob. "Number two is clean and ready, Captain. I'll send my son, Arthren, up with the water. Just ask if you need anything else."

"How much do I owe you?" Edward asked as he fished his purse from a waistcoat pocket.

Cadan and Tobias exchanged glances before Cadan said, "Half a crown will cover the room, a couple of ales, and breakfast in the mornin'."

"Seems more than fair," Edward replied, wondering if he was being treated differently from other visitors to the village. He passed over the coin and turned to Tobias. "I hate that you have to wait—"

"Don't fash yourself. I have business with Cadan here. Take your time."

Edward nodded and made his way up the wooden stairs to the first floor. The room with a number '2' painted in gold paint proved far better than he was expecting, the bed made up with a thick quilt and even a pillow in an embroidered covering. The shaving mirror appeared unused, as did the other furnishings. A Turkish carpet covered most of the wooden plank floor, and thick drapes hung on either side of a window overlooking the water.

The place wasn't new—the architecture was obviously from a couple of centuries earlier—but it had definitely been updated.

He hadn't even opened his valise before there was a knock at the door. "Come," he called out, turning to see a rather well-developed young man holding a steaming bucket of water. His face, ruddy from spending time out-of-doors and on the water, reminded Edward of a member of his former crew.

"That was fast," he remarked as the water was taken to the dressing table. He dug a coin from his purse and held it out to the young man. "You must be Arthren."

"You can call me Art, Captain," the young man offered.

"Well, Art, I appreciate it."

"Thank ye, sir. If you need anything else, let the barkeep know." His eyes rounded at seeing the coin Edward dropped in his hand. "Although I don't usually work here in the inn, I'll be around until midnight," he added.

"You're welcome." Edward was about to return to unpacking his valise, but then said, "Tell me, do you know how late Miss Bristow stays at her candy shop?"

The young man blinked. "She lives there, sir. Above the shop, so... she's always there."

"Does the shop have posted hours?" Edward asked, not wanting to pay a call past closing time.

"Open until six o'clock, sir."

Edward checked his chronometer, relieved to find it wasn't yet half-past-three. "Appreciate the information," he said, relieved when the young man took his leave and shut the door.

Using a bath linen he found on the dressing table—one that seemed as if it was new and never before used—Edward washed up and changed into a different waistcoat. Frowning at how his dark hair appeared tangled, he ran a comb through it before checking his reflection in the shaving mirror.

He didn't wish to scare Miss Bristow. Deciding only a bath would completely erase the odor of travel, he headed back down the stairs to the public room.

Now more crowded, he discovered Tobias seated at a trestle with no fewer than three others sitting with him.

Apparently his title wasn't a deterrent for the locals to drink with him.

"Gentlemen," Edward said as he stopped at the end of the trestle.

"Captain Poulsen. Do join us," Tobias said as he indicated the seat next to him. "We're all equal here," he added as he waved his hand to indicate those that sat with him.

A guffaw sounded from two of the men, their homespun linen shirts and woolen trousers suggesting they were laborers. The other was better dressed, but when he grinned at Tobias' comment, it was apparent he had lost most of his teeth.

A pint of ale was set before him before he had taken a seat at the trestle, the apple-cheeked young woman avoiding his gaze.

"These three are some of our most prolific fishermen," Tobias said by way of introduction.

"We do our best fishing at night," one of them said proudly.

"Depending on the season," another chimed in.

"Is it true you'll be bringing brandy?" the third asked.

"It is," Edward acknowledged. "I'm heading over to the candy shop after this, to confirm everything."

Quiet settled over their table, and Edward dared a glance at Tobias. "Was it something I said?" he asked lightly.

"We're all quite protective of Miss Bristow," Tobias replied. "She wants desperately to make a go of the candy business—she's quite good at making comfits and caramels—but the Bristows only really make a living at Christmastide."

"Do they ship their candy to shops in London?"

Edward asked, remembering how happy he had been to find candies on Christmas morn as a child.

"I think Exeter is as far as their candies go," Tobias replied. "But the scotch they let down and colored was quite popular for those who drink the stuff. It's just too far to the distillery, though. Didn't make sense for the owners to transport it so far, so they didn't receive further orders."

"Pity," Edward said. "Which has me wondering how Pendragon Imports expects brandy to be cost effective shipped from here."

The other four exchanged glances of surprise. "Pendragon?" Tobias repeated.

"He's the one who hired me," Edward replied. "Assured me the operation is entirely above board. I deliver two hundred tubs of brandy, and two hundred tubs get transported to..." He stopped, scoffing as he rolled his eyes.

"Go on," Tobias urged.

Edward pinched his lips together. "How much brandy is there after a tub is let down and the caramel is added?"

"About seven... maybe eight gallons or more?" Tobias guessed with a shrug. "Two tubs."

"Dammit," Edward cursed softly.

Tobias patted him on the back. "I think it's rather remarkable that this Pendragon is willing to subject half his brandy to the vagaries of the excisemen," he said with an arched brow.

"What happens to the other half?" Edward asked in a low voice.

Tobias shrugged. "Depends on how he expects to get it out of here, I suppose."

"How would *you* get it out of here?"

The viscount pretended nonchalance. "Depends on where it's going. London?"

Edward frowned. "That's where he's sending the legitimate stuff."

"So... he's probably loading it onto farm carts of some sort. Covered in hay and destined for Bath or Plymouth. Southampton mayhap," Tobias guessed with a shrug.

Furrowing a brow, Edward regarded the viscount for a moment before he said, "So... he'll be smuggling it out of here."

Nodding, Tobias whispered, "Probably."

"And you'll... allow it?"

Tobias sighed as he glanced around at the others who populated the public room of the *Cock and Bull.* "My father turned a blind eye, and I find I must as well. Swain Cove would not exist if not for smuggling." He paused and regarded Edward with a worried expression. "If you're to bring shipments into Swain Cove and expect help from the locals with unloading it and moving it about, you must agree to keep what you know to yourself," he warned in a quiet voice.

Edward gave a start. "Your secret is safe with me, my lord," he stated before he remembered that he was now more than just a captain of his own vessel. He was also a baron. Should he elect to take his father's seat in Parliament, he would be a member in the House of Lords.

But then, so was Viscount Pencarrow.

"Will you go to London for the next session of Parliament?" Edward asked.

Straightening at the sudden change in topic, Tobias regarded Edward with a furrowed brow. "I should," he replied, although his reply didn't hold any enthusiasm.

"I ask only because I learned yesterday that my father and older brother recently died of a fever. It seems I have inherited a barony."

Tobias eyes widened. "Lord Poulsen has died?"

"You knew him?"

"Met him at some of the Season's entertainments," he replied. "Seemed to possess the right sort of temperament for the job," the viscount remarked.

"He was good at negotiating," Edward murmured.

"A word of advice?"

"I welcome it."

"Take his seat. Represent those in your barony, for no one else will," Tobias stated. "Nothing will change if you're not there to see to it." He paused and lowered his voice. "I might take exception to what occurs in Swain Cove if the tariffs that could be collected were actually used to do something good for this country. But as long as Prinny is acting as king, spending the coffers will-nilly on unnecessary castles, and on jewels for his many mistresses, and on wars in far-off lands, that money is better left with those who do the work to keep this country running. To those who must feed their families," he explained.

Edward nodded in agreement. "You'll hear no argument from me," he said.

"Good," Tobias replied. "Drinks are on me," he added as he dropped a few coins on the table. "Come, let's get you to *Caramel and Sons*, where you can meet the sweetest woman in Swain Cove."

Grinning, Edward said, "Because she makes candy?"

Tobias furrowed a brow. "More because she can't help herself," he replied. "But maybe being around all that sugar has something to do with it," he added with a grin.

The two took their leave of the *Cock and Bull*, Tobias pointing out landmarks, such as the town square and the only church as they made their way. Their sole impediment proved to be a gaggle of geese they let pass on Tobias' recommendation. "Damn things bite," he warned as they watched them cross the road.

"Are they yours?" Edward asked, his brows furrowing

when he noticed other villagers were stopping to wait for the birds to pass them before they resumed their walks.

"Supposedly." The viscount's response held an air of humor, which had Edward chuckling.

Once it was safe, they strolled to a quaint two-story, newly white washed wood-sided building at the edge of the village.

The blue decorative wood cut-outs on the fascia and around the edge of the single front window of the shop made it look like the chalets Edward had seen in European villages. He was about to enter when a young boy ran up to Tobias holding out a note.

Tobias opened the note and frowned. "Go on in. I'll take care of this and be back momentarily," he said as he turned and headed back toward the *Cock and Bull*, not waiting for a response from Edward.

The captain turned his attention back to the candy shop, grinning as he did so.

How could he not? Entering a candy shop after so many years since he'd been in one could only mean he'd leave with a handful of sweets.

Or more if he wasn't careful.

AN UNUSUAL INTRODUCTION

Caramel and Sons, Swain Cove

Edward gave Tobias' retreating back a nod of acknowledgement before making his way into the candy store. The door opened easily, its hinges obviously oiled, for no creaking announced his arrival. There was the sound of a tinkling from a tiny bell above, though. He glanced up, expecting to see it hanging on the end of the door. Instead, it had been hung on the other side, out of site.

Suddenly enveloped in the familiar scents of his boyhood's favorite shop—spun sugar, candied nuts, caramel, a hint of mint and anise—Edward inhaled softly.

"I'll be right there," a woman's voice called out from somewhere beyond the wood and glass cabinet that displayed a selection of sweets. He was about to step forward to look more closely at the selection of colorful comfits when the owner of the voice appeared from behind a curtain.

She immediately stopped and stared at him, which gave him an opportunity to do the same with her. Slender and tall and looking as if she'd been standing over a hot stove—a dewy sheen of moisture coated her face—she wore her raven hair in a large bun atop her head. Tendrils that at one time might have been spirals were now wilted, but they still managed to perfectly frame an oval face featuring dark brows, large eyes, and a pert nose. Her cheeks, red from whatever she'd been doing, were a perfect match to her full lips, which looked as tasty as any of the candies that lined the display case.

"Handsome," she murmured softly, one brow lifting as her lips parted in apparent awe.

Edward swallowed. He'd never had a woman address him so, but he found he didn't mind.

Or perhaps it was someone's name, and she mistook his identity.

He was about to introduce himself—Tobias had said he would when he could join them, but it seemed the perfect moment to mention his real name. He didn't, though, when she moved slowly toward him, one arm lifting so her hand could reach his face.

Holding himself still, Edward felt the pads of her fingers touch his jaw. For a moment, he wished he had taken the time to shave when he'd had a chance, for he was sure his whiskers would scrape those fine fingers.

She didn't seem to mind, though, her eyes following her fingers as they moved up the side of his face, across his brow and down the bridge of his nose.

He was reminded of a time when he had watched a blind girl meet his brother for the first time. Henry had stood perfectly still as the daughter of an earl placed both of her hands on the sides of his face, lightly touching his jaw and cheeks as a means of imagining what he might look like. Edward realized he probably appeared much like Henry had at that moment, dumbstruck and hopelessly in love with the girl.

This woman wasn't blind, though. She could obviously see very well, for her next words were, "So blue," obviously referring to his eyes.

He wasn't prepared for what she did next, though, for the finger that trailed down the front his nose touched his upper lip and traced its outline before she stood on tiptoes and placed her lips against his.

Not having been kissed by a woman in... well, he couldn't recall the last time he'd been kissed, so he was glad his body knew what to do. At the moment, his mind wasn't doing a very good job of remembering anything.

It took every bit of restraint he could manage not to simply wrap his arms around her and pull her hard against his body so that she might feel the results of her ministrations behind the placket of his breeches.

Instead, he slowly opened his lips and then used his tongue to separate hers, relieved to hear her soft moan as the pillows of her lips parted. He kissed her, slowly, thoroughly, his arms finally moving around her shoulders as his tongue explored her teeth and mouth.

Her body was soft despite a spine of steel. He could feel the slight bumps of it as he slid an open hand from the base of her waist—he didn't dare move his hand lower —up to the middle of her back and over a shoulder blade and to the nape of her neck. His finger trailed forward along her jawline and then down her neck as she purred in response, her tongue finally tangling with his.

She was nearly pressed entirely against the front of his body when Edward felt the impending arrival of someone. As if the air around them changed to become heavier.

Remembering Tobias was supposed to join him, Edward ended the kiss as quickly as he could, but he captured her hand in his as the door swung open. He lowered his lips to the back of her hand as she suddenly inhaled, obviously brought out of her stupor by the sound of the tinkling bell and the appearance of Lord Pencarrow.

Edward kissed her knuckles before he stepped back and nodded.

"I see you two have already met," Tobias said lightly.

"Actually, a formal introduction would be appreciated," Edward managed to say, surprised he could speak intelligently at that point. His cock was rock hard, and although he had wished he wasn't wearing his greatcoat a moment ago, he was glad it hid the evidence of his arousal now.

The woman's eyes were wide, almost fright-filled, but she acknowledged Tobias with a nod. "Good afternoon, Lord Pencarrow."

Edward practically groaned. She even sounded sweet.

Tobias gave her a nod before he said, "Miss Catherine Bristow, may I have the honor of introducing Captain Edward Poulsen? He'll be transporting the brandy from France for Pendragon Imports."

Catherine? Edward nearly repeated out loud. He had to suppress the urge to chuckle at the coincidence. *Caton* was the French word for Catherine.

"It's very good to meet you..., Captain," she stammered, performing a perfect curtsy as her face displayed a red blush of embarrassment.

"The pleasure is all mine," Edward replied, wincing at his choice of words. He didn't want to embarrass the poor woman any more than she already was. "I thought to make your acquaintance—and your father's—before I deliver the first two-hundred tubs of brandy at the end of the month."

She nodded, but the look of awe on her face made it apparent she was surprised. "From where have you come?"

"Portsmouth. My ship is there now, being painted and outfitted with some new sails." He decided not to mention the real reason it was there—to repair the hole in the hull.

"I must be going," Tobias said. "Please excuse me." He bowed his head to them and then took his leave, not waiting for a response from either of them. Edward wondered if the viscount had paid witness to their embrace prior to his arrival. The shop did have a front window in addition to the one in the door.

Edward watched the viscount depart and then returned his attention to Catherine. "I wish to—"

"I'm terrible sorry."

He blinked. "Whatever for?"

She rolled her eyes. "Must you make this worse for me?" she asked as her dark brows furrowed.

Edward was about to say, "Of course not," but clamped his mouth shut. He took a moment to devise a response. "You obviously thought I was someone else, and truth be told, I didn't mind," he stated. "I haven't been kissed in an age."

Apparently not expecting that particular response, Catherine relaxed. "Thank you for... for not... for not pushing me away when Lord Pencarrow arrived. I can't imagine what he would have thought—"

"He's a gentleman. He would have thought us old friends. Nothing more," he said, not believing a word of what he was saying. "Let us say no more about it and simply get on with why I came," he suggested.

"Yes, let's," she replied with a wan grin. Her eyes rounded. "Oh, I suppose you'd like to see what happens to the brandy?"

Although he had been more interested in learning what was to happen to the *extra* brandy, Edward decided he was curious to see the business' operation. Especially since his initial perusal of the candy shop suggested it wasn't large enough to accommodate two hundred tubs of brandy, let alone four-hundred or more once they were done with the letting down process. "I am, actually," he admitted. "Do you have the time? I am sorry I didn't send word ahead of my intent to pay a call. I think I must have interrupted your work."

"I was just distilling some water," she replied as she moved to the front door and threw the bolt. She turned a pasteboard sign around in the window to indicate the shop was closed. "My father started making it and then seems to have disappeared," she added as she led him back behind the curtain.

"Is he all right?" Edward asked, his gaze sweeping over the accoutrements that made up a small workroom. Besides a center table, there were shelves on three sides filled with all manner of containers—wooden casks, ceramic jugs, lidded pots, and even some glass bottles—all neatly arranged.

"He's probably at the *Mermaid's Rest* having an ale," she replied on a sigh. "He forgets sometimes," she murmured as she checked the flame beneath a pot of boiling water. Glass tubes led from there to where a spout dripped clear water into a ceramic jug.

Edward watched as she moved to a pump to fill another container with water before pouring it into a funnel above the boiling flask. "May I help you with that?" he asked, realizing she was about to lift the nearly full jug of distilled water from the floor.

She seemed uncertain at first, but then said, "If you'd like. It goes on that shelf over there," she said as she pointed to a line of other jugs that looked the same. "Let me put an empty one in place." She hurried to the shelf and lifted a matching ceramic jug from the collection. Moving it so it sat next to the full one on the floor, she gave him a nod, and he pulled the full one from beneath the spout. She had the empty in its place before more than a single drop of water had fallen on the floor.

"Are all of these full?" Edward asked as he hefted the jug onto the shelf, realizing then that the jugs were three-deep. She followed with a stopper and placed it over the small opening.

"All but these," she said as she indicated the rest of the row. "We need more. Many more, but our order from Stoke-on-Trent hasn't yet arrived."

"Seems a long way away for jugs," he commented. "Surely there must be a ceramics company closer than Stoke."

"There might be," she acknowledged, "but Acme Ceramics make the best ceramic jugs," she countered. "We bought these to let down scotch from a distillery near the border, but..." She gave her head a shake as she took hold of a lit candle lamp.

"But what?" he prompted.

"We're too far away. It make no sense to have the scotch brought here for us to do the letting down and add the caramel syrup only to have to ship it back for the rest of its aging process," she replied on a sigh.

"When you say the border, I take it you don't mean the one with Wales?" Edward asked.

"Scotland," she confirmed. "But the test got us the job with Pendragon Imports, so there's that."

"About that," Edward said as he followed her into the next room, obviously the kitchen. A single window provided what little light was left of the late afternoon, while her candle lamp filled in the shadows. Here the sweet molasses scent of caramel hung in the air, and he inhaled deeply. "It's none of my business, really, but Pendragon assured me this operation was entirely legal—"

"Because it is," Catherine stated, using a metal spatula to lift round globs of caramel from a flat metal sheet into tiny paper cups. "We merely see to the letting down of the brandy and then to adding the caramel syrup," she claimed. "Mr. Pendragon assured us that there would be drayage carts arriving when we had enough casks to send off."

"So… someone *else* will deal with the excisemen?" he asked.

She paused in her work and then sighed. "He said he would deal with them directly, but… your… suspicions are well founded," she admitted. "As a sea captain, you're no doubt familiar with our village's means of surviving."

Edward realized she referred to smuggling, but he ignored her last comment to say, "Pendragon told me two-hundred tubs in, two-hundred tubs out." He crossed his arms.

Rolling her eyes, Catherine seemed uncertain of what to say. "My best guess given the tub he provided for us to use for testing is that there will be two-hundred-and-two tubs more after the letting down process," she admitted. "Possibly a few more, given the volume of the caramel syrup we'll be adding at the end."

Edward glanced down at the caramels she had neatly arranged in a pasteboard box. He didn't know a single woman in London who wouldn't welcome such a treat on Christmas morning—or any morning, for that matter.

"Oh, not these," she said as she indicated the candies. "That," she added as she pointed to a series of clear glass containers filled with a dark liquid. They lined the upper shelves of the kitchen on two sides.

"Caramel syrup?" Edward guessed.

"Exactly," she replied, her surprise evident. "You know about it?"

Edward shook his head. "Only what Pendragon told me," he admitted. "Adds color but no flavor."

Catherine nodded. "We haven't yet determined the

exact amount of caramel to add," she explained. "We don't have a sample of good brandy to match, and apparently the brandy will darken some more when it's put into the oak casks for shipment." She covered the pasteboard box of caramels with its lid.

"Is Pendragon providing the casks?" Edward asked.

Catherine didn't immediately answer but moved to open the next door in what was proving to be a long building. "We had to add another room with its own exterior door at the back," she said as she indicated the storage room. "But Mr. Pendragon paid for its construction. Gave our local carpenters something to do for an entire fortnight, and we gained a sitting room in our quarters upstairs."

Edward boggled at seeing stacks of oak casks lined up all the way around the room, six or seven deep in some spots. The exterior door was directly across from the door he stood next to, and he realized there was probably a road behind the end of the building that provided access for a cart or a wagon.

"Have they been used before?" he asked, pointing to the casks. He sniffed the air in an effort to determine if there was a scent other than oak.

"For wine, apparently," she acknowledged. "They're stained on the inside, but he said that was necessary."

"Good roof?" he asked as he looked up to the ceiling, not having noticed when he had approached the building from the street.

"Indeed. In fact, you can't tell where the old building stopped and the new one starts," she claimed. "The carpenters matched the roof and all. We gained a room in our living quarters upstairs. And they even added some... well, I don't know what they're called, but they look like furbelows one finds on a fancy ballgown. I'm told it makes us look like a right proper candy shop in Paris."

He grinned, thinking she should be the mistress of a candy shop in Paris. With her knowledge and her skills, she certainly didn't belong in a small town such as Swain Cove.

"I should probably meet your father before I head back to Portsmouth," he murmured. "Do you know when he'll return?"

She shook her head. "He loses track of time. At least I know he'll eat something if he's at the *Mermaid*."

Edward glanced around the kitchen, noting there was no evidence of a supper in progress. "What about you?" He remembered how slender she felt in his arms, and now, in the light from the candle lamp, her collar bones were evident beneath her pale skin.

Grimacing, Catherine seemed hesitant to respond. "I'm sure I can find something in the pantry," she replied. "It's only been a few days since market."

"If you show me the way, I could escort you to the *Mermaid's Rest*," Edward offered. "In the company of your lady's maid, of course. Treat you and your father to dinner. As a thanks for the time you have spent with me this afternoon," he added, deciding he rather liked her company. "I didn't mean for you to close your shop on my account."

Catherine looked as if she didn't know what to say. "Oh, it's all right. We rarely get customers in the late afternoon," she finally replied. "Children always come with their mothers after their luncheon for the candies or comfits." She inhaled and added, "As for dinner..." She paused, obviously tempted. "Yes, I will show you the way. I need to turn off the flame to the water and find a shawl." She pointed toward a set of stairs in one corner of the kitchen. "I'll just be a moment."

While she headed up the stairs, Edward went back to the distilled water apparatus, stunned to discover the jug on the floor was nearly full. He pulled an empty one from the shelf and positioned it as she had done and then pulled the full one from beneath the spout. Then he lifted the full one into place on the shelf before searching for a stopper. He found a drawer full of them, all neatly lined up in rows. He was putting it into place when he heard Catherine descending the stairs. A quick glance in her direction had him freezing in place.

Although he had had never met her before that day, he had the oddest sense that he had paid witness to what he was seeing at some point in his life.

Mother, he realized. *Descending the stairs in their Mayfair townhouse, looking ever so elegant.*

"The jug was nearly full, so I switched it out," he said when Catherine appeared in the doorway.

"Careful, Captain, or you shall find yourself with a new position," she teased.

"Jug switcher," he said in response, his huge grin sobering when he realized she had changed her drab gown into something far finer—a deep red dinner gown topped with a multicolored silk shawl. "You didn't need to change clothes on my account," he murmured.

"Oh, but I did. I so rarely go out after dark," she replied, hurrying to extinguish the flame under the water flask.

"And your lady's maid?" he asked, his gaze going towards the stairs.

"She only exists in my imagination, and apparently in yours," Catherine replied as she stepped forward to join him.

With the rays from the setting sun leaving long shadows in the shop, the only light in the room was that from a candle lamp. He held out his arm. "Then let us hope that you shan't be the subject of too much gossip," Edward said.

From the expression she aimed at him in response, he had the distinct impression she wouldn't mind the gossip.

They took their leave of the candy shop and made their way to the *Mermaid's Rest* by the waning light of the setting sun.

CHAPTER 8

A WALK AWAKENS THE SENSES

A few minutes later

"How long have you been a sea captain?" Catherine asked as they made their way along the dirt path toward the *Mermaid's Rest*. It was farther from the shop than the *Cock and Bull* tavern. Farther away than most all the businesses in the small village. As for his concern about any gossip that might result from their trek together, she almost wished they would be seen. This time of the day found most of the villagers huddled in their small homes, sitting around rough wood tables whilst eating their suppers.

"A bit over four years," he replied, his voice rising to be heard above the breeze coming in from the cove. "I was a first mate prior to that."

"On the same ship?"

He chuckled. "Yes. The *Caton*," he replied. "I just bought her at auction, so I own her now."

"*Caton*?" Catherine repeated in surprise, remembering how her mother called her by the diminutive name when she was young. "Isn't that... French?"

"For Catherine, yes," he acknowledged with a

chuckle. "She was captured from the French many years ago, but the British Navy kept the moniker when they put her into service, I suppose as a means to taunt the enemy. Now that I'll be in business for myself, I thought to rename her *Black Cat*."

Catherine wondered at the sense of disappointment she felt at hearing his words. Apparently it showed on her face, because Captain Poulsen was regarding her with an odd expression. "What is it?" she asked, well aware the slight wind had her legs outlined in the skirts of her gown. She had pulled on only one petticoat, not wanting the slim lines of the dinner gown ruined by extra fabric.

"Well, now that I've been kissed by a real Catherine, I'm thinking perhaps I won't change her name," he murmured.

Catherine inhaled sharply, and she was about to apologize again when the captain slowed his steps and then stopped. From the way his gaze quickly raked over her windswept figure, she knew he was seeing the shape of her hips and legs.

"May I know who this Handsome is that I resemble so much?" he asked in a quiet voice. He stood so close, Catherine could feel the warmth of his breath, of his body, as he suddenly blocked the wind. "I don't mean to vex you, but curiosity has me thinking I may come face to face with him at some point, and I should like to—"

"You won't," she interrupted, attempting to resume their walk. The captain held his ground, though, and Catherine realized she would have to tell him the truth. "He's merely a figment of my imagination, sir," she explained, once again feeling the heat of embarrassment color her cheeks. She was glad that twilight had fallen over the village, turning most colors to shades of gray.

Edward's eyes narrowed. "You imagined *me*, but... we've never met," he murmured.

"Exactly," she acknowledged. "So..." She allowed a shrug.

"You think me handsome?"

Catherine inhaled softly before she once again made eye contact with him. She thought perhaps his query was made in an effort to tease her, but even in the growing gloom, she could see his expression. She knew he was serious. "Of course I do. Any woman would..."

The rest of her response was cut off when his lips captured hers, when his arm moved behind her back and pulled her so close her front was pressed against his.

His kiss was nothing like the one they had shared in the candy shop. Although that one had seemed so intimate, what with his tongue tangling with hers, it had been slow and sensuous, gentle and genuine, curious and kind.

This one was far more violent in its passion. His tongue didn't invade hers, but it may as well have. For a moment, she thought to push him away—someone could be watching—but she knew she would forever regret it. She might never again be kissed so passionately, so completely. She wasn't even sure she was standing of her own accord. She couldn't feel anything below her thundering heartbeat and the slight throbbing at the apex of her thighs.

When his hand moved to cover one of her breasts, she didn't back away but pressed her body closer to his. Thrilled at the sensation of his thumb as it coaxed her nipple into a tight bud behind the fabric of her dinner gown.

Never before had she imagined that a kiss could be so intense. So all consuming. She didn't want it to end. So when she sensed he was about to pull away, she mewled her disappointment.

Edward ended the kiss at the same moment he slid his

hand from her breast to her back. He didn't pull away, though, but rested his forehead against hers. His warm breaths, sounding almost labored, slowed before he placed a hand on the back of her head and pulled it against his shoulder.

Awareness came back to her slowly. She was still standing of her own accord, but there was nothing between their bodies but their clothes. A hard ridge pressed into her hip, one she realized was his arousal. The thought nearly had her panicked.

"I apologize—"

"Please don't," she said, her cheek pressed into the small of his shoulder. From what she could see beyond his body, she realized they were sheltered on one side by the cliff. The cove lay below, the noise of water lapping at the sandy shore and the wind the only sounds.

"You'll be ruined."

"I don't care," she countered, almost too quickly.

He stepped back so their bodies were finally apart. "I do," he said.

From the way he said the simple words, Catherine knew he meant it. "Please don't regret having kissed me," she pleaded.

He shook his head. "All right. I won't. But let's get you inside." His gaze darted to her bodice where the silhouettes of her nipples were evident behind the satin fabric. He desperately wanted to cover both with his hands, with his mouth, and he nearly cursed out loud. He hadn't experienced such erotic thoughts in a very long time. "This breeze is growing colder, and I'm famished." He held out his arm.

Catherine was about to argue that it was only cold because they were no longer standing close, but she placed her arm atop his. "I am hungry, too," she admitted, hoping he understood the double meaning in her words.

She was indeed hungry for food, but his kiss had awakened a hunger in her that she'd only experienced in the wee hours of the morning. A desire to hold a man close. To kiss him. To make love with him until the sun lit the sky.

Aware his gaze was on her as they made way their down the inclined path, she said, "Why name your ship *Black Cat?*" she asked. "It will make you seem like a pirate."

Edward chuckled. "I suppose it's not a very original name for a ship bringing goods into a town that makes its living from smuggling."

Catherine didn't react as he was expecting, her gaze going to the water below. "I'm sure I wouldn't know," she replied. "I rarely see ships in Swain Cove. The shop is too far from the water."

"But you're well aware of the smuggling that goes on?" He knew she did. She had practically admitted it back at the shop.

She nodded. "Oh, yes. Everyone who lives here knows of it, even if it is kept well-hidden. Doesn't mean we all agree with it, of course."

"What is your father' opinion?" he asked.

Catherine narrowed her eyes. "He's never said."

"Why did he open a candy shop in such an unlikely place? Such a small village?" Edward asked, wondering if perhaps the shop was somehow involved in smuggling in a manner other than liquor.

"Probably because it was unlikely," she replied lightly. "No possibility of competition. More possibility of opportunities, such as the one with Mr. Pendragon." She paused before she added, "And it was my stepmother's home. She wouldn't leave, and he wouldn't give her up."

Edward scoffed. For some reason, he had thought the

candy concern was relatively new to Swain Cove. "So you weren't born here?"

She shook her head. "My mother lived in Exeter. Father had a confectioner's shop there, and Mother decorated tea cakes and made biscuits. That's where I was born. We lived there until Mother died a few years ago."

Edward furrowed a dark brow. "Your stepmother...?"

"Died last year. They were only married two years, thank the gods," she murmured. "She was not a pleasant woman. Treated my father rather poorly."

"Treated you worse," Edward guessed.

She scoffed but didn't deny his words. "And yet Father misses her. Drinks too much. Forgets things."

"You worry about him."

She glanced up at Edward as they made their way. "I do. He's my protector. He has the money from my stepmother's dowry. My dowry," she murmured. "If something should happen to him—"

"You will still have a protector," Edward stated as he opened the door to the *Mermaid's Rest* and stepped aside.

Catherine inhaled softly, but she didn't ask what he meant as she entered the inn.

Not when she spotted her father.

CHAPTER 9
DINNER PROVES AWKWARD

*P*retending the past fifteen minutes hadn't left him aroused, confused, and entirely off-kilter, Edward opened the door to the *Mermaid's Rest* and motioned for Catherine to step in.

He watched her enter, watched how she carried herself. She seemed different from when they had left the candy shop, her slender frame straighter, her chin held higher. The blustery breeze from the cove might have tousled her bun and the tendrils of hair that framed her face, but the sight of her reminded him of that moment when she had descended the stairs into the kitchen.

That moment when he was reminded of watching his mother come down the stairs in their Mayfair townhouse. Head held high, spine straight.

Regal.

Men might have controlled every other aspect of life in London, but his mother ruled Poulsen House. She might have only been a baroness, but she was its queen, and although he hadn't met any of the other women in Swain Cove, Edward was fairly sure Catherine Bristow was its queen.

So how could he have been such a bounder and done what he had? Kissed her, out in the open, for anyone to see? Held her in a lover's embrace? Palmed her breast and kneaded it as if he had the right?

One thing was for certain.

Catherine Bristow was no fresh-from-the-schoolroom miss. She was a woman. Older than he had first thought. Beautiful. Capable. Responsible.

Far more so than her father, who was passed out on one of the trestles in the taproom of the *Mermaid's Rest.*

"Oh, Father," he heard her say as she moved to stand behind him. She leaned over one of his shoulders, a hand gently shaking him until the old man jerked and straightened on the worn wooden bench.

"Och, dammit, daughter," Franklin groused as he glanced about. "Just restin' me eyes, is all." His rheumy gaze went first to her manner of dress and then to Edward. His bushy brows furrowed. "Who might you be?"

"Poulsen," Edward said as he held out his right hand. "Captain Edward Poulsen. I'll be bringing the tubs from Pendragon Imports at the end of the month. It's good to meet you, sir."

Franklin stared at the hand a moment before he shook it, the knuckles of his smaller hand gnarled from arthritis. "Poulsen, you say?"

"Captain Poulsen is treating us to dinner, Father," Catherine said as she caught the attention of the waiter. She moved to the other side of the trestle and took a seat as Edward moved to join her.

"Where you from?" Franklin asked, his manner still suspicious.

"London, originally," Edward replied. He had barely been aware of anyone else in the taproom when they arrived, but now he noticed the clientele that sat at small tables around the perimeter of the small room. Most all were men, bronzed from the sun and probably younger than they appeared. *Fishermen*, he thought, before the waiter appeared with a round of ales. The pungent odor of sour hops assaulted his nostrils. "But I've been in the British Navy for the past ten years. Came here straight from Portsmouth."

"Navy?" Franklin repeated. He took a long draught from his mug and set it down on the wood planks.

"Yes, sir. I bought my own ship, and Pendragon Imports is my first client," Edward explained.

"So, what are you doing here?" The old man's query was filled with suspicion.

"Father," Catherine gently scolded. "He came to meet us. To learn about our operation," she said before turning to Edward. "You'll need to let him know what you'd like brought for the meal," she said in a quiet voice as she indicated the waiter.

"Oh, of course," Edward said as he waved for the server to return. When he did so, Edward asked about the food.

"We got fish stew, some cheeses, pasties, and mutton pie. Bread, o' course."

"More than usual," Franklin muttered, sounding cynical.

"Do you have wine for the lady? Claret, perhaps?" Edward asked. He couldn't imagine Catherine drinking the sour ale.

The server blinked. "We do, but you'll have to buy the whole bottle, sir."

"Of course," Edward agreed. "And we'll have the stew and... well, just bring some of everything," he added, his stomach grumbling. When the waiter left their table, Franklin asked if Edward had other business in Swain Cove.

"No other business," he replied, "but I took a room at the *Cock and Bull* for the night." Realizing Bristow wouldn't be satisfied with more, he decided he could mention Theodosia. Surely having family in the area would help his case. "My aunt lives nearby, so I spent some time with her prior to coming here."

Catherine regarded him with surprise. "Where does she live?"

"St. Austell. I left her with her... with her paramour, I suppose you'd call him," he stammered, deciding Catherine was old enough to understand his meaning. "She's agreed to marry the man, but something about her manner makes me think she's not as serious as he is about the parson's mousetrap," Edward said with a grin. "Perhaps you've had dealings with him. Timothy Christianson?" he added, curious as to how she would react. "He introduced himself as an exciseman."

Despite keeping his voice low, the conversations around them seemed to quiet suddenly, and Edward realized some in the room were eavesdropping. Well, he was a stranger, so he couldn't fault anyone for their suspicions.

"He did the paperwork for our last shipment of candies to Exeter," Catherine murmured, obviously bothered at hearing the name. "Ruined several of the boxes of caramel. I had to hurry back to the shop and prepare replacements. Thank goodness I had enough candies made up, or we might have lost our contract with the shop in Exeter."

"Why would he do such a thing?" Edward asked in alarm.

Franklin exchanged quick glances with his daughter before he said, "Thought we was trying to smuggle something, he did."

Edward scoffed. "What did he expect to find?"

Catherine shrugged. "Jewelry, gemstones, tea, playing cards, cigars—"

"Soap, salt, butter, or chocolate," Franklin murmured.

"Lace and fabric. The boxes were too small to be liquor, of course, but that's what they look for the most," Catherine said on a sigh. "Given we're so close to the French ports."

Edward stiffened on the bench. "Then I hope Arthur Pendragon has a plan for the other half of his brandy," he murmured.

Franklin grumbled something about excisemen and took a swig of his ale.

"I do hope you found your accommodations acceptable?" Catherine asked, obviously uncomfortable with the topic of brandy given those who sat around them.

Edward nodded. "I do. Very much. In fact, I wonder if anyone has ever stayed in room number two before me? Everything in there seems new."

Catherine froze in place, surprised he would mention that particular room. She had heard it was reserved for only the very best guests of the *Cock and Bull*. "The Thomases have always been good innkeepers," she offered. "Derwa—Mrs. Thomas—is very fastidious with regard to the rooms. With their cleanliness."

"I met her son today," Edward commented. "He seems amiable."

"As is her daughter, Morwenna," Catherine said. "She's several years younger than me, though." She paused a moment. "Might I be so bold as to ask where you will go when you leave here?"

Although he thought he might have read more into her query than she intended, Edward found he welcomed her curiosity. "I have to find a ride back to St. Austell on the morrow. Catch the mail coach to Portsmouth." He paused. "When I return at the end of the month, I'll be on the *Caton*."

"Perhaps there's a ship going that way," Franklin suggested. "Probably first thing in the morning," he added, his attention on two windows that faced the water.

Edward followed his gaze, his brows furrowing when he didn't see anything but reflections of the interior of the taproom. A far away light blinked beyond the glass, though, followed by another. A few in the taproom stood and dropped coins on their tables before they departed. After another minute, two more took their leave.

"I don't suppose those men were going home to their suppers?" Edward guessed as the waiter set down several bowls and a pot of stew. As Catherine ladled the stew into the bowls, an older woman left them with some spoons and serviettes and then placed a bottle of wine in front of Catherine along with a glass.

"Probably not," Catherine whispered. She moved the bowls into place. As she did so, Edward could see movement beyond the windows, dark figures heading toward the water.

"How often do ships come into the cove?" he asked as he poured her a glass of wine, nodding to the server who returned with a loaf of bread.

"Depends," Franklin replied. "When the weather is good, sometimes two or three a week."

"There are enough men here to handle that many... goods?" He had almost said contraband, but thought better of it.

"There are," Franklin affirmed. "I'd join 'em, but..." He held up his hands. "Not as strong as I used to be." He turned his attention to his soup and began to eat.

"I suppose it will be a late night for most of the village?" Edward guessed.

"We rarely hear the fishermen at the shop," Catherine whispered. "The hiding places for their catch are... well, they're well hidden," she added, an eyebrow arching in a teasing manner.

Edward grinned and ate his soup, happy to see how much Catherine seemed to enjoy the wine. "Is it any good?"

She nodded. "I haven't much to compare it to, but it is far better than the ale."

"Good," he said, helping himself to some of the other food the server had delivered.

They ate in companionable silence for most of the meal, and when they had finished, Edward ordered port for Franklin and himself and then refilled Catherine's glass.

"Port?" Franklin said in surprise. "Haven't had port since..." He let the sentence trail off. "Well, since we lived in Exeter, I suppose."

"It's a proper way to end a meal," Edward remarked. "But I will admit it's been awhile since I've had it." He turned to regard Catherine, noting how her cheeks were reddened from the wine. She seemed content. Happy, even.

He couldn't remember a time since he lived in London when he had sat next to a woman for a meal.

The oddest sensation gripped his chest.

He thought of their kisses. Remembered how her body had felt pressed against his. How she had allowed him to plunder her lips and caress her breast. How she had caressed his face before kissing him back at the shop.

His cock certainly remembered. The damn thing was taking up every bit of available space behind the placket of his breeches.

If only...

He shook the thought from his head. They had only just met. He couldn't expect she would join him in his bed that night.

Perhaps when he returned in a fortnight.

CHAPTER 10
A TALK IN THE DARK

An hour later
Edward offered his arm and escorted Catherine back to the candy shop while her father, carrying a lantern, preceded them. His bent back suggested he had spent part of his life laboring in the fields.

"His parents were tenant farmers," Catherine murmured. "My mother's family had a confectionery, which is how he got into the business," she explained.

"Do you like it? Making candy?" Edward asked, placing his free hand atop the one she hooked around his arm as they made their way up the inclined path. Given the breeze from the cove, the air was becoming chilly. He expected she might use her other hand to move his, but instead she seemed to accept his action as an invitation to walk closer to him.

"I've never known anything else," she replied. "I can't imagine what I would do for my living if I wasn't making comfits and candies. I do know that if I didn't have it as my avocation, I would have to do what all the other women in this town do."

"Which is?" Edward prompted.

"Whatever it takes to support their men in the business of smuggling." Her gaze went to the water, where fishing boats dotted the surface on their way to or back from the ship that was now anchored in the middle of the cove.

Edward nodded his understanding, realizing her words were the first to imply the entirety of Swain Cove existed for the sole purpose of smuggling. "Have you ever thought of... leaving? Going somewhere else?" he asked, keeping his voice low.

She scoffed. "Where would I go?"

"London," he replied.

Inhaling softly, Catherine regarded him a moment. Although she couldn't see him well in the dark—there was barely a moon and the lantern's light was directed at the path ahead—she knew he was watching for her reaction. "I've no one there. No one I could stay with," she replied.

"If there was. If..." He sighed.

"Who do you know there?" she asked, her brows furrowing.

He scoffed, but realized it had been a long time since he'd been in the capital. "My mother, my sister, her husband... *me*, at least for a while when I finish this job for Pendragon Imports," he said.

"I assumed you were going to live on your ship," she replied. "At life on the sea."

"I was. I will. Just... not *all* the time," he stammered. "I learned the day before yesterday that my father and brother recently died," he admitted, struggling with how his throat thickened at the reminder of his aunt's words. Despite having been away from his family most of the past ten years, he would miss his brother.

She inhaled softly. "You learned this from your aunt?" she guessed.

"Indeed."

"I'm so sorry for your loss," she murmured. "So now you have responsibilities in London?" she surmised. "To your family?"

"I do," he admitted on a sigh. "I won't have to live there all the time, but I should during the Season."

"So you can be a privateer the rest of the time," she reasoned.

He chuckled. "That's the new plan," he said, feeling relief at having sorted what he would do going forward.

When they reached the candy shop, he had half a mind to kiss her. Given her father's presence, he thought better of it and merely kissed the back of her hand.

"Will we see you before you depart tomorrow?" Catherine asked as her father opened the door.

Edward inhaled, wondering if he could be so bold as to leave it up to her. "I truly hope so, Miss Bristow. Good night."

He bowed and headed toward the *Cock and Bull*, well aware Catherine watched him until the night swallowed him whole.

CHAPTER 11
A FATHER SURPRISES

few minutes later
"He's sweet on you," Franklin remarked when the candy shop door was closed and the tinkling bell had come to rest. He lit a candle lamp for her from the flame in the lantern.

Catherine pretended indifference. "He's not at all what I expected, given he's a ship's captain," she replied.

"An officer in the military is the highest rank for a gentleman," her father countered. "And Captain Poulsen knows how to treat a woman. I watched him during dinner. Ordering wine. Pouring it for you. Escorting you all proper like. Ye'll never do better, Cat."

Blinking at hearing her father's claim, Catherine moved to follow him through the workroom and into the kitchen. "What are you saying?" she asked, shocked by the implication in his words.

"If he asks if he can court ye, I'll give him my permission," he replied. He headed for the stairs.

"But... but what about the business? The shop?" They had a contract with Pendragon Imports to let down one-thousand tubs of brandy. Besides that, they had more ceramic jugs on order so they could expand their business.

"Ye needn't worry yer pretty little head about it none. Once this business with Pendragon is finished, so am I. Retirin', I am."

Catherine blinked. "When did you decide this?" she asked in alarm, feeling as if a rug had been pulled out from beneath her. Making candy and running the shop was all she knew.

"Ye deserve better than living with an ol' crotchety man like—"

"Father!" she scolded.

"Don't ye be Fatherin' me," he countered. "Biggest mistake I ever made was takin' ye from Exeter. There ye would have had yer pick of a dozen young men. Here... well, I can see the captain likes ye. Ye'd have to be blind not to notice how he looks at ye. Like he wants to kiss ye. Even Pencarrow noticed." He waved at her gown. "Ye must have, too, since you dressed up for him all proper ladylike."

"Lord Pencarrow?" she repeated in disbelief, ignoring his last comment. "He was only here..." She sucked in a breath, remembering when the viscount had come to the shop earlier that afternoon. Perhaps Tobias Pencarrow *had* seen her kissing Captain Poulsen before he entered the shop.

"He might be a viscount, but he's one of us, and he knows what's what 'round here. And if he says ye're Captain Poulsen's woman, well, then, ye are."

Catherine leaned her back against the kitchen door jamb, stunned by her father's words. Stunned that Lord Pencarrow would make such a claim.

She should have been incensed at the thought that someone she barely knew would say such a thing. As if she had no say in the matter.

But she wasn't.

Not one bit.

"You would give him my dowry?" she asked. She knew he still had her late stepmother's dowry. He obviously intended to live on it during his retirement.

Her father straightened. "I would. When he gives you a ring, I will," he vowed.

Catherine inhaled softly. "He'll be back in a fortnight," she said quietly. "If what you say is true, then he'll pay a proper call on us." She sighed, her gaze going toward the front of the shop.

She knew that half of the village was down at the water's edge, the men standing shoulder-to-shoulder as they passed barrels and crates from one man to the next as each fishing boat came to shore and was unloaded. Most of those barrels and crates would end up hidden beneath the *Cock and Bull* for safe storage, while some would be loaded directly onto carts and hauled off in the dark.

The ship that brought them might spend the night anchored in the cove, but sometime in the morning, when the tide was right and the winds came from the west, it would probably sail up the Channel.

Edward might end up on that ship as it made its way north. But for now, he was in the best room at the *Cock and Bull*.

Room number two.

"I'm going to bed, Father," she said as she moved to follow him up the stairs.

"I'm headed there meself," he replied. "Somethin' to be said for being too old to help out with the unloadin' down at the beach."

Catherine watched him head into his bedchamber and close the door before she headed into hers.

As she slowly undressed, she remembered Edward's last words.

I truly hope so.

Inhaling softly, she decided his words weren't meant for the following day.

They were an invitation. One she decided she would accept.

CHAPTER 12
A CAPTAIN NEEDS A MATE

eanwhile, at the Cock and Bull
Pretending to ignore the increased activity on the far side of the *Cock and Bull*, Edward entered the inn and was about to head up to his room when the innkeeper's son called out to him.

"Are ye in need of anything, Captain?"

Edward paused, not about to admit what he really wanted—Catherine Bristow, naked and warming his bed —but he realized a bath might help his situation. "Is there any hot water for the bathing tub?" he asked.

"Of course, sir. I've got two pails of water on the stove, too. I can put a couple more on. Would you like me to bring them up?"

"I would. Say fifteen minutes?"

"Very good, Captain."

Edward grinned as he watched the young man head into the kitchens. Then his gaze went to one of the only two men in the taproom.

"Lord Pencarrow," he murmured as he moved to join the viscount.

"Captain Poulsen. How was your dinner?" the

viscount asked as he lifted a mug to his lips. He took a sip of the ale.

"I was so hungry, I don't know," Edward replied with a chuckle. His gaze went to the windows that faced the water. "Quite an operation they have going on out there," he remarked.

"I wouldn't know. I'm pretending it's not happening," Tobias replied with a smirk.

"Probably for the best," Edward agreed, his thoughts on the coming few weeks. "Any chance you know the captain of that vessel? If he's headed north, I'm hoping I can catch a ride."

Tobias nodded his head to a table at the back of the taproom. "If you'd like, I can introduce you," he offered.

Stunned, Edward followed the viscount's line of sight and then scoffed. "Thanks, but I think we've already been introduced," he said in surprise. He headed to the other captain's table. "Jacobs?" he asked, recognizing the naval officer.

"Poulsen? I don't see you for years, and then I see you twice in a week's time. What the hell are you doing *here?*" Paul asked as he stood and shook hands with Edward.

"You wouldn't believe me if I told you," Edward replied. "I don't mean to interrupt your evening, but I was wondering if you might be headed north in the morning?"

"I am. Back to London. Where's your ship?"

"Portsmouth, having a hole in its hull repaired, but I have to go to London for a week or so."

"Everything all right?" Paul asked as he motioned for Edward to take a seat.

"Not exactly. I learned Father died, as did my brother, Henry, so I want to go see how Mother is doing," he replied as he took the proffered chair.

Paul's eyes rounded. "Oh, dammit, Poulsen. I'm so

sorry," he murmured. Then his eyes widened even more. "*Lord* Poulsen," he added. "You are the spare heir, are you not?"

Nodding, Edward said, "I am. Which means my plans to be a privateer have been changed slightly. If I'm to do my duty, then I'll only be able to sail the *Caton* when Parliament isn't in session."

Paul scoffed. "You'll have to get married. Sire an heir," he said in mock horror.

Although he had already come to the same conclusion, Edward hadn't yet decided when or exactly how that was going to happen, but he had someone in mind to be his baroness. "Any chance your... cargo... included any jewelry?" he asked in a whisper. "Any rings?"

Angling his head to one side, Paul reached into one of his pea coat pockets and pulled out a hinged box. "Funny you should ask," he replied as he glanced about before opening the box. Five rings were lined up, stuffed into velvet beds. "Got them as a bonus for transporting the liquor," he whispered. "See anything you like?"

Edward scoffed as he stared at the jewelry. Three of the rings were far too ostentatious to be wedding rings. One was a large silver band and obviously made for a man. The last was a gold band with a ruby solitaire.

Remembering Catherine's dark red gown, he plucked the ruby ring from its bed of velvet. "How much do you want for it? And for the passage to London?"

Paul closed the box and sat back. "Actually, I could use some help at the wheel," he countered.

"Everything all right?"

Shrugging, the other captain said, "I'm short a first mate, is all."

"What happened?" Edward asked in alarm.

"He fell in love with a French girl and stayed in Havre, the bastard." Paul rolled his eyes as Edward chuckled. "I know where I can find one in London, though."

"I'll be happy to help," Edward replied. "What time do you want me on board?"

"I'm not going until noon or so. The winds should be good by then," Jacobs said.

Edward grinned. "I'll join you at ten or eleven. No later." He held up the ring. "I have a proposal to make."

Paul chuckled. "Found your baroness already, you did?" he asked, obviously humored.

"I think she found me, actually," he replied, noticing Arthren carrying two pails of steaming water up the stairs. "That's my bath," he added. He held out his right hand. "See you in the morning."

Paul shook his hand. "At least I won't have to smell you," he replied with a grin as Edward headed toward the stairs. "See you tomorrow."

CHAPTER 13

A PLEASANT SURPRISE IN THE NIGHT

A half hour later

Rising from the copper tub, water sluicing from his body, Edward helped himself to one of the bath linens Arthren had brought with him on this last trip up the stairs.

He wasn't sure what he had said or done to have the proprietor of the *Cock and Bull* assigning him to the best room in the inn, but Edward wasn't about to complain. Even the bath linen seemed fresh and new.

He had given the boy a sovereign for his troubles before asking if the tap would be busy later that night. Once the cargo from the ship was completely unloaded or carted away, he thought there would be a number of thirsty men invading the taproom.

"Pro'bly not, Captain. Most of the villagers will head to their beds," Arthren said. "Which means you shouldn't be bothered by any noise from down below."

"Very good," Edward replied, watching as the boy gave him a nod and let himself out of the room.

Impressed at how the water stayed warm during his bath, Edward realized then that it was on the hearth of bricks directly in front of the fire. With any luck, it would stay warm for his morning ablutions.

Wrapping the linen around his lower body, he was about to head to the bed when he heard a quiet knock on the door. Thinking it was Arthren, he opened it and sucked in a breath.

Garbed in a hooded cloak, Catherine stood staring first at him and then at his bare chest.

For a moment, neither said anything. Then Edward seemed to awaken from his stupor and pulled her into the room. He quickly closed the door. "You came," he said in a whisper of awe.

"Forgive me, but I was sure when you left us that..." Catherine's whispered words halted as her gaze once again swept down his body and back up to his face. She reached out with a bare hand, her fingers barely touching his chest before she quickly pulled them away. "Well, I thought you... I thought you might be expecting me," she stammered on a sigh of embarrassment.

Edward captured the hand and pulled it to his lips. "I would have come for you in the morning," he whispered. "If you hadn't come tonight."

Her eyes rounded. "So... you *did* invite me?"

His massive arms were around her even before his lips took hers in a crushing kiss. He ended it quickly, though. "What of your father?" he asked.

"He's asleep," she murmured. "It took me longer to leave because I had to wrap the door bell with some fabric to keep it from making any sound when I left."

Edward chuckled before he tightened his hold on her. "How long can you stay?"

Catherine inhaled softly. "For how long will I be welcome?"

His amusement was not only audible, but his body

quaked in her hold. "The rest of my life," he finally replied, sobering as he said the words.

Her eyes rounding, Catherine stared at him a moment before she said, "I should go back at dawn. Most in the village will still be in their beds."

"You do know what I'm going to do to you tonight?" Edward asked as he rested his forehead on hers. "You'll be mine, Catherine. Thoroughly ruined. No one else can ever have you but me."

She swallowed at hearing the implication.

She would be his mistress.

She could expect nothing more. He was a ship's captain. He would be away far more than he would be in Swain Cove. "I understand," she whispered, surprised at the sense of disappointment that settled over her.

His breathing becoming labored—just holding Catherine had every nerve ending buzzing with anticipation—Edward said, "I'll speak with your father in the morning."

Catherine gave a start. "What? *Why?* He doesn't need to know about this," she whispered.

Edward narrowed his eyes. "Of course he does," he said as he removed her cloak. "I'm going to be your protector."

Stunned to discover she wore only a shift beneath her cloak—it was then he noticed she carried a small valise—he took it from her and set it on a chair. "Clothes for the morning?" he guessed.

She nodded, her face blooming with color. "I've never done this before," she whispered. "Please don't think me fast."

Sighing, Edward stood before her and allowed a wan grin. "I do not," he replied. "I am, however, very glad you came."

"You bathed," she said, noticing the citrusy scent that

surrounded him and then the copper tub on the hearth. She lifted a finger to his jawline.

"And I shaved," he said. "I wanted to be clean for you."

The oddest sensation shot through Catherine just then. Frissons of anticipation and delight had her knees feeling weak. "Will you teach me what to do?"

His lips captured hers once more before he slowly pulled away and nodded. "You only need to be willing," he whispered. "I'll see to your pleasure first, of course." Lifting her with an arm beneath her bottom, he carried her to the bed and set her on the edge, coaxing her knees apart so he could stand between them.

Given the condition of his manhood—his cock throbbed with need of her—the bath linen he wore around his middle fell away. He managed to grab it, tossing it onto the counterpane as he pressed his hips into the edge of the high bed.

He didn't want her to see his arousal lest it frighten her.

"May I touch you?" she asked, her voice sounding breathy.

"Of course. Anywhere you'd like," he whispered as he placed his hands on either side of her face. He tilted her head back and kissed her thoroughly, his tongue briefly tangling with hers before his lips trailed down her neck and to her collarbones, along the edge of the shift and finally onto one breast.

She whimpered when his tongue swept over the fabric-covered nipple, which had him moving his attentions to the other breast. Before he could capture it in his mouth, though, the fabric that covered it moved up. He pulled away to find Catherine struggling with pulling the shift up and off of her body.

He inhaled sharply when the white muslin sailed through the air and landed somewhere beyond the bed. His gaze settled on her bare breasts a moment before he lifted it back up to her face. "By the gods, you're gorgeous," he breathed.

"It was in the way," she murmured on a huff, referring to her shift. Suddenly feeling far too exposed—she was completely naked—Catherine had half a mind to cover her breasts with an arm. But his comment had her feeling emboldened. Beautiful. Excited and aroused.

Her attention had once again gone to what she could see of his torso. Even in the dim light from the fireplace, she could tell he was bronzed from the sun, his chest covered with a sprinkling of dark curls that thinned to a line that trailed down his stomach and then was hidden by the edge of the bed. She reached out and slid her hand over his chest and down to his ribs, feeling as well as hearing the hitch in his breath. "Your skin feels hot," she murmured.

"No doubt," he replied before he reached out with both hands and pushed her shoulders until she finally fell back on the bed.

She gasped as he lifted her knees over his shoulders. Gasped again as his tongue left a trail of moisture on her inner thigh. Nearly screamed when it darted between the delicate folds between her thighs.

Something down there was throbbing. Pulsating with a need she had never felt before. Leaving her wet and ready for something to fill a void she didn't know she possessed. Demanding a surcease she didn't understand. "Oh, please," she whispered.

His answering chuckle had warm breath spreading

over her quim. "Give me a moment, my sweet Caton," he whispered.

Given her position on the bed and her lower legs resting on his back, she had no means of anchoring herself in place. She could only grasp handfuls of bedding as his tongue swept over and around her swollen womanhood. Sharp darts of pleasure mixed with a rolling rapture culminated in a joy so intense, she was sure she was floating away. The joy only intensified, as if a wave carried her along before it finally, blessedly, left her pleasantly exhausted and sobbing.

She was also in a completely different position on the bed, her head on the pillows and Edward hovering over her, his bath linen beneath her bottom.

"Lift your knees to my sides," he whispered, his breathing labored.

She did so, surprised she could even make any part of her body move. Something heavy came to rest on her quim, long and heavy, which sent another dart of pleasure racing up her spine as it then moved along her folds, pressing on her already sensitive core.

Above her, Edward grimaced. "This may hurt a bit," he said before the tip of his cock settled at her opening.

Catherine felt the nudge, felt the slow invasion come to a stop before he pulled out. "What's wrong?" she whispered.

"Shh, nothing, my sweet," he responded before he plunged his cock into her on a grunt. "I'm so sorry," he managed to get out as he stilled his body. He kissed one of her nipples but otherwise didn't move. "From what I hear, it shouldn't hurt after this," he added as he moved his lips to her other nipple and kissed it.

Inhaling sharply at the sudden sensation of fullness in her lower body, Catherine held her breath a moment. "Why are you sorry?" It didn't hurt, exactly, but there had been a moment of discomfort. "I'm all right." At the same moment she said it, she lifted a hand to the side of his face. "Please, don't stop."

He kissed her lips at the same moment he pulled almost all the way out of her, moaning at how tight she had felt around him. Thrusting into her, he groaned and lifted his chest higher. "Hang onto me," he whispered.

But Catherine had already moved her hands to his back, gripping him as she felt the muscles of his back bunch and then relax with his every thrust. She arched her back, lifting her chest in a desperate attempt to feel his chest rub over her breasts.

Her change in position had Edward cursing softly before his entire body seemed to cease its movements, his cock buried deep inside her. His head lifted, his eyes closed, and the cords of his neck showed in relief. She inhaled sharply when she felt a rush of heat bloom through her lower body at the same moment he growled.

"Oh, you minx," he scolded on a chuckle before he lowered his body slowly to hers, his breathing labored.

Catherine wondered if she had done something wrong, but his words hadn't held any censure. She was about to ask, but her attention went to how he was struggling to wrap one arm around her upper back and another behind her bottom.

"Hang onto me," he managed to say as he rolled off of her, bringing her body along so it rested atop his once he was on his back.

Catherine stifled a cry of surprise at the sudden change in their positions. "Are *you* all right?" she asked, worry evident in her voice.

He chuckled again, joy softening the harsh planes of his face. "Better than I have been in a very long time," he replied. "Oh, I'm going to love coming home to you," he added, as one of his hands moved to the back of her head to pull it down to the small of shoulder. Her raven hair fanned over his chest like a curtain of silk, and he closed his eyes on a sigh.

Finally relaxing atop Edward, her knees on either side of his hips, Catherine could feel his manhood still firm inside her, although the sense of fullness it had caused was no longer so foreign. Little by little, she took stock of her body, her senses more acute than usual. Every nerve ending seemed more aware. Had it been lighter in the room, she was sure colors would seem brighter.

So when Edward put voice to a question, his voice seemed loud. She gave a start and lifted her head from his shoulder to stare at him.

He blinked. "I know you have more water to distill and such, but I'd really like for you to come with me tomorrow."

"To London?"

"Yes. I have some family business I need to attend to before I head back to Portsmouth. From there, we'll sail to Cherbourg-en-Cotentin, load the tubs of brandy, and be back here in Swain Cove in a fortnight." He knew the schedule was aggressive—he might only have three or four nights in London—but it would give him enough time to meet with his father's solicitor and settle any issues. Spend some time with is mother. Maybe procure a marriage license.

"How would we get there?" Catherine asked, straightening her arms so she hovered over him.

"On *Destiny's Fate*," he replied, his attention going to where her breasts pressed into his chest. He swallowed.

Catherine ignored the odd sensation that was occurring deep inside her—Edward's manhood seemed to be filling her once again—and asked, "What is *Destiny's Fate?*"

"The ship that's out in Swain Cove. I know the

captain. He was a fellow naval officer, and he's in need of a first mate for his voyage to London."

Straightening so she was sitting up atop Edward, Catherine inhaled softly. "When is he leaving?"

Edward's hands moved to her hips and slid up her sides and to her front to cover her breasts, his expression showing appreciation. "Apologies, but what did you ask?"

Giggling, Catherine covered his hands with her own. "Bounder," she accused.

"Noon," he said with a huge grin. "I told him I would be aboard at ten or eleven o'clock. That will give us plenty of time for breakfast, and for you to pack a trunk, and for me to speak with your father."

Catherine sobered, reality forcing second thoughts to the forefront. Although she was excited about an opportunity to go to London, she knew she couldn't. Travel on a ship with a man she hadn't even known a whole day? Without a chaperone? Anyone who saw her would assume she was a... well, she didn't know what they would think, but it couldn't be good.

All because she had allowed an almost stranger to ruin her. Thoroughly.

She couldn't fault him.

She had been the one to kiss him first.

She had been the one who allowed him to kiss her out in the open when they were on the cliff, for anyone to see, even if it was dark.

She had been the one to show up at his room, late at night, wearing only a shift beneath her cloak, her hair loose from its pins.

When his body jerked beneath hers, one of his arms reaching towards the nightstand, Catherine asked, "What is it?"

He captured something in his hand and resumed his prone position. The sight of him, beneath her like this, his beautiful body stretched out on a dark velvet counterpane and his expression suggesting he was enjoying himself, had her wishing they could do this every night, which only reinforced her thoughts that she had become some sort of harlot.

"I hadn't planned to do this now. Not like this," he said as he gazed up at her. "I was imagining doing it by the water's edge. Or on my ship," he murmured.

"Do what?" she asked in a whisper.

He took her left hand in his free hand and then slid the ruby ring onto it as she watched in shock. "I haven't asked your father yet, but I will in the morning. Catherine Bristow, will you be my wife?"

Catherine stared at the ruby ring, flames from the fireplace reinforcing the facets in the red gem. "You wish to marry me?" she asked in awe.

"I do," he replied, sobering at her reaction. "I wouldn't have kissed you if I didn't feel affection for you."

Her eyes rounded. "Affection?" she repeated.

"Well, of course," he said with a grin. "Why else would I kiss you?"

She continued to stare at the ring. "I thought you wanted me to be your *mistress*," she said with a roll of her eyes.

"Well, I'd want that, too," he admitted, understanding now why she had seemed despondent at first. "Surely you came here wanting to be more than a mistress, though?"

She nodded. "I wasn't sure. At least, not until my father told me I should be glad of your arrival today. He noticed your attentions during dinner, you see. Noticed what I wore."

"As did I. Thought the ruby would go well with your dinner gown," Edward murmured as he brought her hand to his lips to kiss the back of it.

"He wants me to marry a gentleman. Wants you to be

my husband," she said as she tore her gaze from the ring and leaned down to kiss him on the lips.

"Does he now?" Edward asked when she pulled away.

"He does," she affirmed.

"Well, that will make my conversation with him in the morning a bit easier," Edward murmured. "So, there's just one other issue I must discuss with you."

Catherine stiffened, and then let out a squeak when he pulled her down and off of him. She mewled when his manhood left her body, and then she frowned when she saw the seriousness of his expression as he turned onto his side and held his head up on a crooked elbow. "Oh, dear," she whispered.

"When I told you about my father and my brother, I didn't tell you why their deaths have affected my situation. My plans for how I wished to live the rest of my life," he murmured.

"You mean as a privateer?" she whispered.

He nodded. "I can still be a privateer part of the time," he clarified. "But I must be a baron all of the time—"

"Baron?" she repeated. "Baron Poulsen?"

"—Lord Poulsen, which means you will be Lady Poulsen. All of the time," he warned. "My mother will help. She'll introduce you at Society events. Make sure you're invited to *soirées* and such. Afternoon teas and garden parties."

She scoffed. "You make it sound so awful," she teased.

"Because to me it is," he countered. "But once they get a taste of your caramels, you'll be on the guest list of every aristocrat's wife in London," he went on, hoping it would be that easy for her.

"Will I be allowed in a kitchen, do you suppose?"

"You'll have your own," he stated.

Her eyes rounded. "My own kitchen?"

"At Poulsen House," he affirmed.

Catherine stared at him in disbelief before she giggled. "Am I dreaming? Of course I am. I'm having a dream about Handsome, and he's asked me to marry him," she murmured as she sobered.

"God I hope not," he replied. "For then I would be dreaming as well." He kissed her nose. "Will you come with me? To London?"

She nodded. "I will."

He kissed her nose again. "I want nothing more than to make love to you again."

Her eyes rounded. "Then why don't you?" she asked, frissons darting through her at the reminder of what they had done earlier that night.

"Because you're probably… sore," he replied.

"I'd want to bathe, of course," she countered.

"The water is still warm," he whispered.

Before he quite knew what was happening, Catherine rolled off the bed and hurried to the tub. Edward had barely sat up when he watched her, silhouetted in the flames of the fireplace, lower herself into the copper tub.

"Oh, this feels so divine," she whispered in delight.

Edward chuckled, joining her with the intent of helping.

He may have been more than a hindrance, but Catherine didn't mind.

CHAPTER 14
EPILOGUE

Six months later

     "That's the last of it," Catherine said as she added caramel syrup to a tub of brandy.

Arthur Pendragon watched from where he stood leaning against the kitchen door jamb. "Are you quite sure I can't talk you into doing this for a thousand more tubs of brandy, my lady?" he asked on a sigh.

Catherine giggled as her father saw to sealing the tub. "The Season starts in a fortnight," she replied. "And I have every intention of attending every ball and *soirée* until this baby makes it impossible for me to do so." Her hand went to her middle, where only a slight bump was evident.

"And I'm officially retired," Franklin stated as he straightened from his task. "I'm too old to do this," he added as he waved around the *Caramel and Sons* workroom.

"Surely you have a buyer for the business?" Pendragon argued.

"A young couple has agreed to take over," Catherine replied. "They're locals, but they've learned everything I can teach them about making caramel, candies, and comfits."

"What about caramel syrup?" Pendragon asked hopefully. "Distilling water?"

Catherine and her father exchanged knowing glances. "That, too," Franklin said on a sigh, pulling a paper from a waistcoat pocket. "Names and where you can find them until they take over the business next week."

Arthur Pendragon fisted a hand as he took the note from Franklin. "Thank the gods," he said, his gaze going to Edward when the ship's captain joined them in the workroom.

"All the cargo is finally off the *Caton*," he announced, grinning at seeing his wife presiding over a dozen tubs of brandy. "No thanks to the exciseman, Timothy Christianson. The bloke took inventory of every one of the crates we off loaded," he added.

"Oh, dear. How much trouble did he give you, darling?" Catherine asked in alarm.

"Well, I think he was going to ask for a bribe until I reminded him he's my uncle. He and Aunt Theodosia married a few months ago."

"Helps to have family in the right places," Franklin muttered.

"Indeed. Anything I can do to help here?" Edward asked, his gaze going around the workroom. The shelves were once again filled with ceramic jugs, now all empty of their distilled water.

"We're done here," she replied. "Take me to dinner, Lord Poulsen?"

"You read my mind," Edward replied as he moved to kiss her. "Westerly winds will favor us in the morning, so I've reserved a certain room at the *Cock and Bull* for us this evening," he whispered as he waggled his brows.

"Bounder," she accused with a huge grin.

Both Arthur and Franklin turned away, embarrassed at the couple's display of affection.

"Do they do this often?" Pendragon asked in alarm.

"Always," Franklin replied. "Has me deciding to take another wife, though."

"Do you have one in mind?" Pendragon asked.

Franklin nodded. "She's meeting me at the *Mermaid's Rest* tonight. Joinin' me for a pint of ale." He waggled his brows.

Pendragon raised a brow. "Well, good luck with that," he remarked.

"Good night, Father. I'll come say to 'good-bye' in the morning," Catherine said before she kissed her father on the cheek.

"I take it you're all packed?" he asked, sobering.

She nodded. "Edward has everything but my valise loaded on the *Caton*. We'll leave in the morning."

"You'll come back when the Season is over?" he asked, his manner guarded.

"We will," she affirmed. "When I expect you'll be introducing me to my newest stepmother." She rolled her eyes and huffed in feigned dismay.

"And you'll be introducing me to my grandson," Franklin countered.

Catherine gigged. "That, too," she replied. "Or a granddaughter," she added, giving both her father and Edward a mischievous glance.

"She'll be as sweet as candy," Edward murmured. "Whereas a boy…" He grimaced. "I imagine I'll be consuming comfits as fast as you can make them," he teased.

ABOUT THE AUTHOR

A self-described nerd and student of history, Linda Rae spent many years as a published technical writer specializing in 3D graphics workstations, software and 3D animation (her movie credits include SHREK and SHREK 2). Getting lost in the rabbit holes of research has resulted in historical romances set in the Regency-era as well as Ancient Greece.

A fan of action-adventure movies, she can frequently be found at the local cinema. Although she no longer has any tropical fish, she follows the San Jose Sharks and makes her home in Cody, Wyoming.

For more information:
www.lindaraesande.com
Sign up for Linda Rae's newsletter:
Regency Romance with a Twist
Follow Linda Rae's blog:
Regency Romance with a Twist